The Notorious Wolfes

A powerful dy...
and so...

TH...
Eight siblings, blesse... ...
one thing they wan... ...ve. A family
destroyed by on... ...'s thirst for power.

THE SECRETS
Haunted by their past and driven to succeed,
the Wolfes scattered to the far corners of the globe.
But secrets never sleep and scandal
is starting to stir....

THE POWER
Now the Wolfe brothers are back, stronger than ever,
but hiding hearts as hard as granite.
It's said that even the blackest of souls can be
healed by the purest of love....
But can the dynasty rise again?

**Each month, Harlequin Presents® is delighted to
bring you an exciting new installment from
The Notorious Wolfes. You won't want to miss out!**

Eight volumes to collect and treasure!

Cara sipped her champagne and watched Jack.

"I found a deck of cards," she said as she took the bottle over and poured him another drink. "Why don't we play a hand or two of poker?"

His gaze swung toward her.

"I know you're used to winning," she said, "but you've never played me. I'll try not to embarrass you, though."

Jack couldn't resist a challenge. "What are the stakes?" he asked, and her heart soared. She'd intrigued him enough to shake him from his brooding.

"If I win, you take me to some awful touristy thing that I'd love, but you hate."

He almost grinned, she was certain. "And if I win?"

Cara shrugged. "We go somewhere you want instead."

"Doesn't sound like much incentive," he said, taking a sip of the champagne.

His eyes narrowed, his gaze slipping over her body. Any second and he would know the effect he was having on her.

"I have a better idea," he said as his eyes met hers again.

"What's that?"

"We play for the clothes on our backs. Or we don't play at all."

Lynn Raye Harris

THE MAN WITH THE MONEY

 **Harlequin®**

TORONTO NEW YORK LONDON
AMSTERDAM PARIS SYDNEY HAMBURG
STOCKHOLM ATHENS TOKYO MILAN MADRID
PRAGUE WARSAW BUDAPEST AUCKLAND

Recycling programs
for this product may
not exist in your area.

ISBN-13: 978-0-373-23788-3

THE MAN WITH THE MONEY

Originally published in the UK as THE HEARTLESS REBEL
First North American Publication 2011

Copyright © 2011 by Harlequin Books S.A.
Special thanks and acknowledgment are given to Lynn Raye Harris for her contribution to The Notorious Wolfes series

All about the author...
Lynn Raye Harris

LYNN RAYE HARRIS read her first Harlequin® romance novel when her grandmother carted home a box from a yard sale. She didn't know she wanted to be a writer then, but she definitely knew she wanted to marry a sheikh or a prince and live the glamorous life she read about in the pages. Instead she married a military man and moved around the world. She's been inside the Kremlin, hiked up a Korean mountain, floated on a gondola in Venice and stood inside volcanoes at opposite ends of the world.

These days Lynn lives in North Alabama with her handsome husband and two crazy cats. When she's not writing, she loves to read, shop for antiques, cook gourmet meals and try new wines. She is also an avowed shoeaholic and thinks there's nothing better than a new pair of high heels.

Lynn was a finalist in the 2008 Romance Writers of America Golden Heart® contest, and she is the winner of the Harlequin® Presents Instant Seduction contest. She loves a hot hero, a heroine with attitude and a happy ending. Writing passionate stories for Harlequin is a dream come true. You can visit Lynn at www.lynnrayeharris.com.

Books by Lynn Raye Harris

Harlequin Presents®

2986—THE DEVIL'S HEART
2925—THE PRINCE'S ROYAL CONCUBINE

Many thanks to Sarah, Caitlin, Abby, Robyn, Janette, Jennie, and Kate for making this project so much fun to work on! The only thing that could have made it more fun was if we'd had a writers' retreat somewhere tropical while we worked. Maybe next time....

CHAPTER ONE

CARA TAYLOR wiped sweaty hands against the tight satin of her skirt, hoping she didn't leave an imprint. Tonight was the night. The biggest night of her career as a croupier thus far, and she'd just been dealt a blow she wasn't sure she could recover from.

Bobby wanted her to throw the game. Cara took a deep breath to steady herself. She could do this. She *had* to do this. The men who would arrive at her table in just a few minutes were some of the wealthiest, most daring men in the world. In many ways, though they made her job possible, she loathed them. They were accustomed to waging millions of dollars on one turn of the cards, and just as accustomed to losing as they were winning. This was child's play for them.

Did it matter if she was the instrument of their losses tonight? Not one of them would go home poor. Not one of them understood what it was like to lose everything they had, to fight and struggle for survival on a daily basis.

Cara knew. She'd been fighting to save her family since Hurricane Katrina blew through New Orleans over five years ago and devastated their home. And not only their home; Katrina had also blown away the diaphanous veil obscuring her father's dark secrets. With her father's betrayal and her mother's subsequent breakdown, it had been Cara's responsibility as the oldest to make sure her family was safe and well. It had taken a long time and a lot of work—not to mention putting her own dreams on hold—but she'd gotten them back on their feet.

Tonight, she finally had a chance to put financial worries behind them for good. She would set Mama up with enough money to make sure the house was paid for and the exorbitant insurance premiums covered. Since the hurricane, insurance companies had raised their rates through the roof. And Mama didn't want to move farther inland.

Though it often frustrated Cara, she also understood it in a perverse way: New Orleans was home. Mama had been born and raised there, and she couldn't leave it. Nor, it seemed, could Cara's sister, Evie. She chewed the inside of her lip. If not for Evie staying home to help Mama and their little brother, Remy, Cara wouldn't be here. And since she was here, she owed it to them all to do everything she could to secure their future.

After tonight, Remy would continue to have the specialized care he needed, which was the most important consideration of all. The bonus Bobby had promised her when she'd agreed to come to Nice for the opening of his new casino would finally enable her to achieve all the goals she'd had when she'd left home.

But first she had to throw this game.

"You understand what you have to do," an oily voice said from behind her.

Cara turned smoothly, hoping her distress didn't show on her face. "Of course."

Bobby Gold winked as he tapped her on the ass. Cara did her best not to flinch. She'd never liked Bobby, but he was the king of the casinos in Vegas—and abroad, as this new multi-billion-dollar facility located in an old French palace in the center of Nice proved.

When she'd begun working as a croupier, it had been for one of Bobby's rivals. It hadn't taken long for Bobby to find her and offer her a job. She'd refused at first—but money, and her desperate need for it, had eventually won out. And, other than the occasional leering pass from the man, she'd had no reason to regret her decision.

Until now.

Bobby's gold tooth caught the light as he smiled.

She'd never been sure if it was an affectation, or if the man really needed a gold tooth. Nevertheless, it disgusted her.

"Keep the players happy, Cara. Use those beautiful breasts of yours to distract them as much as possible. And keep an eye on the man I point out to you. When the stakes get high enough, he'll give you the signal."

Cara's face burned, but whether from Bobby's casual suggestion she use her breasts to distract the players or from the idea of cheating—of going against her entire moral compass—she wasn't quite sure. She suspected it was a bit of both. Cheating wasn't in her lexicon, especially after the devastation her father had caused. Adultery was a different kind of cheating, but the results were the same. It was simply wrong.

And she wasn't a cheater, period.

Cara slid a nervous hand down her skirt once more. She wanted to pull her shirt closed a bit more, but she wouldn't do so while Bobby leered at her. Usually, her uniform consisted of a long skirt and a high white-collared shirt with a bow tie.

Tonight, Bobby had given her a new uniform. Short, tight black satin mini, and deep-V crimson silk blouse. The bow tie was still a part of the uniform, only now it was around her bare throat.

Just get through tonight, Cara, and you can go back home and never see Bobby Gold again.

A pang of wistfulness shot through her at the thought of leaving Nice before she'd even gotten to explore it. She'd put her dreams of adventure on hold after Katrina's devastation, and now that she'd finally gotten to go somewhere wonderful, she was about to leave again.

"I'll do what I can, boss," she said.

Bobby's face grew hard, his gaze cold and cruel. She'd seen that look before. A shiver washed over her at the thought of all Bobby was capable of.

"Make sure that you do, Cara. I'd hate to have to punish you."

Before she could answer, he turned away and strode toward the bar. Cara let out a long breath. She turned back to the table as the black velvet curtain to the private entrance parted. A tall blond man strode into the room and went straight for the bar. She could hear his accent as he ordered. German. Count von Hofstein, then.

As the minutes trickled by, several more men entered the luxurious room that Bobby had set aside for this very special game. A fat sheikh, who wore a headdress with his three-piece suit and sported a huge ruby ring on the index finger of his left hand. An African man, tall and handsome with luminous ebony skin, came in and took a seat at the table. One by one, the seats filled.

The men were quiet, contemplating the game perhaps.

When there was only one chair left, the curtain parted again and another man entered. Cara's pulse kicked up. He was tall, lean and impeccably dressed in a bespoke tuxedo. His hair was dark—black or brown—and his eyes were the most piercing shade of silver she'd ever seen. His jaw was strong, handsome, his lips almost cruel in their sensuality. Everything about him screamed money.

And everything about his demeanor said he didn't give a damn about anyone or anything.

Cara shivered as a chill prickled down her spine. She'd never had quite this reaction to the sight of a man before. She'd moved with her ex to Las Vegas, but she hadn't done so because her heart had fluttered when James had entered a room.

This man's expression, so cold and distant, grew even chillier as he looked at her. She quickly glanced away, cursing herself for staring.

Great. He probably thought she was one of those women working in a casino in order to snag a rich husband. She'd had more than one man assume she was looking for a good time, but she'd quickly set the record straight whenever any of them assumed she was up for sale along with the poker chips.

A touch on her arm startled her, and she jumped, her heart slamming into her ribs. Bobby pulled her away from the table. Cara folded her arms over her breasts, hating the way Bobby looked down her shirt, and hating that he knew it bothered her by the way he grinned at her.

"Don't get any ideas of being noble, Cara," he said. "That bonus I promised you will go a long way toward helping your sweet mama, so make sure you remember it." He leaned in close, ran a fat hand down her arm. "The man with the red tie is Brubaker. When it's time, pass the play to him. He'll take care of the rest."

"Yes, boss," she said, hoping her revulsion didn't show.

Cara returned to the table and took out her deck of cards. After announcing the rules of the game, she shuffled. Then she passed the deck to the player on her right, who also shuffled. After a series of shuffles and cutting the deck, Cara dealt the cards.

The man with the silver eyes was directly across from her. He picked up his cards. There was no flash of emotion, no indication whether he was pleased or irritated, before he set them back down. During her time in Vegas, she'd seen her share of card sharks and amateurs. She'd always been able to tell what a player thought of his hand by the telltale little signs she'd observed at countless tables.

But this man was unreadable.

Until he looked up and caught her gaze. His eyes bored into hers, and her pulse skittered wildly. For the first time tonight, she was glad she wasn't wearing a high collar. Because she'd have been sweating beneath this man's gaze if she had been.

His mind did not appear to be on the cards lying in front of him. Slowly, his gaze slipped over her, lingering on her breasts, before sliding back up. His regard didn't repulse her the way Bobby's had. No, if anything, her skin tingled with awareness and heat.

Cara dropped her eyes to the green baize of the table. She had to concentrate on this game, had to be prepared to perform her task when the time came. She didn't have the leisure to gape at gorgeous men.

Gorgeous, useless men...

Jack Wolfe thumbed the cards he held and waited for someone to call. He hadn't spent time at a card table lately, but when he'd heard Bobby Gold was opening a casino right here in Nice, where Jack had been spending a great deal of time for his business lately, he'd been unable to resist.

He and Bobby didn't know each other well, but

they went back a long way—and not a moment of it was pleasant. Bobby never missed an opportunity to spew his rhetoric about lazy, inbred British aristocrats and their inability to manage their money. Jack knew it was a dig at his long-dead father, and though he couldn't care less what manner of disparaging things anyone said about that sorry excuse for a human being, Jack couldn't turn down the chance to beat Bobby at his own game.

Jack didn't frequent casinos—the stock market was far more challenging—but tonight was a special case. He'd once gone head-to-head with Bobby in a game of chance. It hadn't even been serious, just a random event set up by one of Jack's friends who'd been telling Bobby that Jack was a whiz with cards. Bobby, as a new casino owner at the time, had been unable to resist. And when he'd repeatedly lost everything, he'd grown angry.

Yes, Bobby Gold was a mean brute of a man. Jack didn't need the money, but he would certainly enjoy watching Gold's fat face turn purple when he won the jackpot. He'd thought Gold might try to keep him out of the game, but the man merely nodded at him. It made Jack wonder what Gold had up his sleeve.

Cards weren't a challenge at all, not any longer. It had been years since Jack had enjoyed a game, but he'd never lost the ability to read those around him. And he never would. Reading people was second nature to him. Growing up, he'd needed to be able to tell what someone—his father—was about to do based on the twitch of a muscle, the tick of an eyelid or the jerk of the lips. Then, it had been a survival skill. That it was also a skill which translated to the card table was something he'd found out much later.

These days he preferred the high stakes of stock trading, the rush when he made a killer deal and the satisfaction of doing it all again just a short while later. The sums were much greater, the thrill much more intense. And the need to read people, still very necessary, was relegated to determining the behavior of the pack.

Jack looked up at the croupier again and lifted an eyebrow when she glanced away nervously. The instant he'd walked behind the curtain and seen her standing there, in her little top and even littler skirt, he'd felt like the evening would be much more interesting than he'd originally anticipated.

He'd watched with interest when Gold had taken her away for a word. Her body language was defensive and her face closed off, though he'd thought he'd seen a flicker of unease in the way she'd swept her long hair off her shoulder. When Bobby leaned in and ran a hand down her arm, Jack had to stifle the urge to leap across the table and punch the man in the face.

As the hand finished and the sexy croupier called the first break in play, the men got up from the table and filtered to various corners of the luxuriously appointed room. Some whipped out cell phones while others chatted quietly.

Jack didn't move. He stretched out his long legs beneath the table and took a sip of his drink. Mineral water with a twist of lime while he was playing. He didn't drink alcohol when he needed his senses to be sharp.

The croupier straightened the chips with quick movements. Jack found himself mesmerized by the elegance of her long-fingered hands, the way she seemed to caress the chips before letting them go. He imagined those hands on his body and was instantly glad he'd decided to remain seated.

A waiter stopped at the table, round tray held in one hand, towel over his arm. "Would you like something from the bar, sir?"

"No, thanks," Jack said. "How about you?" he directed to the croupier.

The girl looked up then, her green eyes wide. She truly was extraordinary, from the long dark hair flowing down her back to the high round breasts beneath her obscenely suggestive shirt to the longest damn legs he'd ever seen. What would those legs feel like wrapped around him later tonight?

"N-no, thanks," she said, her voice throaty and

musical—and surprisingly shy, he thought. She'd had no such problems when she was calling the play or rapping out the rules to disgruntled players. It intrigued him, fired his blood.

"I don't bite," he said lightly.

She glanced down again, then back up, her gaze fixing determinedly on him. A tiger, this one. "Whether you do or not isn't the issue, *monsieur*. I'm not allowed to accept drinks from the guests while on duty."

"Then perhaps when you are off duty."

He didn't think she was aware that she'd bit her full lower lip. "I don't think so."

"You'll be off duty then," Jack pressed.

"I don't know you," she replied. "But I'm certain by your presence at this table that we don't have anything in common—"

"How can you say that? I play cards, you deal cards. Much in common, I would think."

Her lovely throat worked as she swallowed. There was frost in her voice. "That's not what I was talking about and you know it. Unlike the money on this table, I'm not up for grabs."

Jack laughed. She had spirit, this woman. He liked that. He held out his hand. "Jack Wolfe."

He didn't think she would accept, but she gave his hand a quick squeeze before snatching hers back. His palm tingled where they'd touched.

"Cara Taylor."

"It's nice to meet you, Cara Taylor. *Very* nice."

She didn't answer him, but a red flush crept up the creamy skin of her neck. Before he could say anything else, the players filtered back to the table, taking their seats and tucking away phones and PDAs.

Once they were settled, Cara dealt a new hand. Jack loved the way her fingers moved, loved the way she seemed so in control and calm when overseeing the game. It contrasted with the tartness of her tongue and that shy vulnerability she'd displayed when he'd been flirting with her. She was an enigma, this woman, and one he intended to explore in great detail later tonight.

He had no doubt she would succumb to his charm. Women always did.

That was part of the beauty of being a Wolfe, even if he despised the name and the man who'd given it to him. Jack knew how to be charming when necessary, and how to be utterly cool at all times. Nothing fazed him.

The play moved quickly, the pot piling up in the center with each hand as the men at the table grew bold. The sleek African drummed his fingers on the table almost silently. It was a nervous habit, and one Jack translated to mean he had good cards but not good enough.

All the better, then.

At that moment, Count von Hofstein's upper lip

ticked up, oh so briefly, in the barest hint of a smile as he glanced down at his hand again. Jack felt a rush of contempt for the man. He was so easy to read, so arrogant and sure.

"Vun-hundret tousand euros," the count pronounced, his accent thick with excitement.

The other men at the table folded, a collective groan rippling over them. The African hesitated a moment longer than the rest, but he, too, threw his cards down. Jack tossed in his chips. "I'll see that and raise you another hundred."

The count's eyes narrowed, but he flung the chips into the center. "Call."

A wave of adrenaline flooded his veins. Jack loved this moment, loved when he unfolded the cards and revealed the winning hand. It was a rush like no other, a torrent of feeling that buoyed him and took away the anger and pain of his past, however briefly.

There was no way he could lose. Unlike the count, he wasn't swayed by arrogance. The count's hand simply wasn't good enough, which the man would have known if he'd been paying attention to the play.

Jack glanced at Cara, saw the knowing smile on her face and wondered how she'd figured it out. Perhaps there was a mathematical mind behind all that beauty, after all.

Jack laid the cards on the table. The count

deflated. Cara's eyes sparkled. "A straight flush," she pronounced. "The gentleman wins."

It had been over an hour since the game began. Cara kept the cards moving, kept the men at the table. The African decided he'd had enough and left, but the rest of the men didn't seem eager to go anywhere. Brubaker, Bobby's ringer, chewed on a cocktail straw, the corners of his mouth tipping into a slimy grin whenever she made eye contact.

The jackpot was climbing to enormous sums. Each hand made the men bolder, the wagers more ridiculous. Jack Wolfe tossed chips into the pot like they were a child's marbles, the gesture careless and unconcerned. He had a nice pile of chips built up beside him, however. She hadn't figured out his angle, but he was very good with the cards.

She'd known professional card sharks in Vegas, but could a man throwing around this much money truly be nothing more than a professional gambler? The thought sickened her, and yet she knew it was possible. He might be wagering for a boss, playing for the profit he would make when he won. It seemed like quite a risk for anyone to take in bankrolling this man, yet since he was good enough, she supposed the possibility of rewards outweighed the risk.

For a while, she'd thought he was counting cards. But he wasn't. He was just that smart at figuring out which cards were left. He folded when his hand wasn't good enough, though he'd also bluffed his way into the win a few times, as well. He seemed not to care, which translated to a high tolerance for risk, she supposed.

He caught her eye, winked. Liquid heat flowed through her even while she chided herself on reacting to him. She had an inner magnet that attracted her to men who were no good for her. When James had taken off with their rent money, and all the money she'd been saving for Mama, she'd sworn never again to get duped by a pretty face and a charming smile.

Jack Wolfe had both—as well as an extra dose of magnetism she couldn't quite put her finger on. But he was the kind of man who drifted from casino to casino, playing cards, living off his winnings, sleeping with the sort of women who frequented casinos looking for rich men.

Someone cleared his throat, and she realized the hand had ended.

"Gentlemen, let's take a fifteen-minute break," she said, her skin feeling warm with embarrassment at getting caught daydreaming.

She moved away from the table, intending to slip into the back for a while and breathe without Jack Wolfe affecting her senses.

"Want company?"

Cara drew up short as he stepped into view. Mercy, he was a handsome man. Tall, dark, with the kind of brooding good looks that could grace a feature film. In fact, he reminded her of someone. An actor she couldn't quite think of at the moment. She hadn't watched a movie in so long that it was no wonder she couldn't come up with a name. That's what working twelve hours a day did for you.

"Guests aren't allowed in the staff areas," she told him.

"Then don't go into the staff area," he replied, the corners of that sardonic mouth turning up in a heart-pounding grin.

What would his mouth feel like on hers? Would those lips be as hard and demanding as she thought? Or would they be gentle, thorough and absolutely addictive?

Her vote went for absolutely addictive no matter what. Not only that, but she could listen to him talk for hours. There was something about a British accent that turned her into a puddle. It sounded so enchanting, as if every British person lived a life of glamour and knew exactly what to do in every social situation. Beside him, she felt small, insignificant. Unpolished.

Cara pushed a strand of hair over her shoulder, willing away the heat, the achiness, this man inspired. "You shouldn't be talking with me, Mr. Wolfe. I have a job to do, and you're a guest."

"But I like talking to you, Cara."

"Only because you think you can score," she said, trying to infuse her tone with acid. It didn't quite work because his smile didn't waver.

"Ah, so now we come to the truth." He set his drink aside, shaking his head at the waiter who hovered. The waiter disappeared. "Call me Jack."

"I'd rather not." Oh, but she would. Repeatedly. She imagined saying his name while they were entwined. The room would be dark, the atmosphere sizzling. She closed her eyes as a bead of sweat dripped between her breasts. Why was she thinking these things? She never did this, never wanted a man she'd only just met. Never wanted to sink into a hot, dark bed with him.

"I think you would," he said, his voice a deep, sensual purr. "You feel this thing between us, too. You want to know more."

Cara swallowed. "You're mistaken, *Jack*. I want to finish this game, and I want to go home and get out of this outfit…" Her words trailed off as the look on his face grew more intense.

"And I want to get you out of that delightful outfit."

Her heart was pounding, thrumming, making her dizzy. "At least you're honest."

"But you aren't." His smile mocked her.

"I admit I find you attractive," she defended, heat enveloping her. Whether it was the heat of embarrassment or the sexual heat of being near this man, she wasn't quite sure. "But I don't know you, and I'm not in the habit of going home with men I don't know."

That was the honest truth, though she was beginning to wonder if she didn't need to let her hair down a little bit. She'd been so uptight since coming to Nice. And now, with the task she faced before this night was through, tension roiled inside her. Maybe a night with Jack Wolfe could relieve the tightness beneath her skin.

So long as he didn't figure out that she was the one responsible for him losing.

"Then perhaps we should get to know each other," he said.

"Perhaps," she replied, surprising herself in the process. Was she really considering this? Or was she letting the flattery of a man like him flirting with her go to her head? Or maybe she didn't know what to say, so she said the first thing that popped into her mind.

No matter what, however, she wasn't leaving with Jack Wolfe. Because as soon as this game was over, she was taking her money and going home to New Orleans. Her conscience pricked her, but what choice did she have?

For Mama, Evie and Remy, she told herself. *I'm doing it for them.*

He took a step toward her, his big body radiating heat and sexuality. She wanted to melt against him, wanted to let the big strong man rescue her. Except that's not what Cara Taylor did. She took care of herself, and she didn't need rescuing. Not ever.

"I look forward to it," he replied smoothly, his silver eyes darkening as his gaze slipped down her body. It was a blatantly sexual look—and she loved it.

What she didn't know was why. "It's time to return to the table," she said quickly, sidestepping him before he could touch her. Because if he touched her, she was afraid she wouldn't have the strength to do what she needed.

She caught Bobby's gaze as she made her way back to the table. His brows were drawn down, his face twisted into a cruel sneer. Her heart thumped for a different reason now. If she didn't do Bobby Gold's bidding, there was no telling what he'd do to her. Money would be the least of her worries.

CHAPTER TWO

IF NOT for Cara, Jack would have gotten bored a long time ago. The cards were too easy, too inconsequential. If he lost, he'd make it back on the stock market. But he wouldn't lose. He never lost. People thought he had the good luck gene in spades, but the truth was he'd learned to rely on his skill with probability and numbers because he had to. Once his father had died, once his brother Jacob had abandoned them—and then Lucas shortly after—the responsibility to take care of his younger brothers and sister had fallen to Jack.

He'd needed to use every resource he had in order to make money, but it wasn't enough. He could take care of his family's finances, but he couldn't heal the open wounds that refused to close. They'd all, every one of them, suffered at the hands of William Wolfe. He'd tried to fix it, but nothing would ever make it right. Annabelle, sweet Annabelle, would carry the scars of what William had done to her for the rest of her life.

Jack shook off the memories of his sister's scarred face and focused hard on the game. This was no time to get lost in thoughts of the past. Fifteen million euros in casino chips were piled in the middle of the table. The sheikh was sweating profusely and Count von Hofstein's brows had drawn into a permanent frown.

Even Cara looked pensive. She was biting her lip again, that luscious lip he longed to suck between his own. Her fingers, so certain and sure as she did her job, were trembling. One of the men at the table, an insignificant man with a red tie he'd recently loosened, seemed to glare at her as if he were trying to impart a telepathic message.

She looked up then, directly at Jack, and his gut clenched. She seemed…uncertain. Her expressive eyes were wide and her creamy skin appeared to have lost a shade of color, making her appear pale and fragile.

"Sir?" she said.

It took him a moment to realize she was talking to him. And that it was his turn.

"Call," he replied, tossing his chips into the pile. Because he was tired of sitting here, because he wanted to get out of the dark, cloying atmosphere of this room and back into the fresh air. Because he wanted to talk Cara Taylor into getting into his car and going for a drive along the coast. He still had a few days before he had to be in London for

Nathaniel's wedding. Spending it in bed with a vibrant woman like Cara seemed a perfect plan.

The man in the red tie, the only player who hadn't folded this round, laid his cards on the table with a smirk. "A full house, Mr. Wolfe," he said. "Queens and kings."

Jack only sighed. "That's excellent." And then he flipped his cards over one by one. Ten. Ten. Ten.

The man's brow glistened.

Jack flipped over the two of hearts and the man sucked in his breath triumphantly, his fingers reaching automatically for the pile.

"Not quite," Jack said as he turned over the last card. The man's jaw dropped.

Count von Hofstein groaned. *"Mein lieber Gott."*

Cara Taylor looked at the last card and smiled. But the corners of her mouth wavered as she did so. "Four of a kind. The gentleman wins."

Jack stood. He didn't feel satisfaction or triumph. He simply felt *done*.

"If you will excuse me, gentlemen, I believe I'm going to cash out."

Cara's fingers definitely trembled as she gathered the cards. Red Tie glared at her furiously before turning to look over his shoulder. A prickle of awareness tingled through Jack. This wasn't good, and yet it was too late to change the outcome. Dammit, he'd known Bobby Gold was up to something.

As if in confirmation of the fact, Bobby stepped from behind a door at the other end of the room. He stopped to talk with one of the bouncers. A few seconds later, the man made his way toward the table. The other players were getting up to stretch their legs, but Jack didn't miss the look on Cara's face when the man stopped beside her and leaned down to whisper something in her ear.

Beefy fingers spanned Cara's upper arm as she turned and walked toward the back of the room with him. Another croupier stepped from the wings—a blonde with fake breasts and a spray tan—and took out a fresh deck.

"Gentlemen," she cooed. "Surely you aren't finished yet. Mr. Gold would like to spot each of you fifty thousand euros as his gift to remain in the game."

Jack's intuition kicked him in the gut as Cara disappeared behind the door Bobby had just exited. He knew what fear looked like, knew the kind of terror an abusive man inspired. He'd witnessed it often enough growing up. Cara Taylor was scared about something.

And he couldn't leave without finding out what it was. He'd been unable to protect his siblings from William Wolfe's wrath, but he'd be damned if he'd let Cara get hurt tonight.

* * *

Cara's cheek stung where Bobby had backhanded her. Blood trickled down her lip from where his ring sliced her. She sat on a small chair in a windowless room and cursed herself for her inability to do what he'd wanted.

But as she'd stood there, looking at the pile of chips in the center of the table, she'd known she couldn't cheat. Mama would be ashamed of her. She would be ashamed of herself. The only thing she had was her integrity. To allow someone else to take that away?

Unthinkable.

And yet she now wished she'd done just that. Because Bobby was furious. He'd hit her and screamed at her and locked her up in here. She didn't know what came next, but she was certain it wasn't going to be pleasant.

She dropped her head into her hands and sat there, waiting. Bobby was ruthless, but she didn't think her life was in danger. And once he got over his anger, he might let her return to the tables. She was very good at what she did, and Bobby knew it. But she wasn't willing to compromise her integrity. She simply couldn't. If they knew where they each stood on the issue, then she could keep working and Bobby would never put her in a position like this again.

Dream on, Cara.

It was impossible and she knew it, but she

couldn't help holding out a small hope everything would work out. If not, then she'd head home and start again. Starting over was nothing new for her. She'd find a way to make it work.

The door opened and her head snapped up. She expected Bobby—and she was ready to try and make him see reason—but the man who entered made her stomach drop to her toes. She shot to her feet, her heart thudding.

"What are you doing here? Get out before Bobby finds you!"

She felt Jack's gaze on her skin like a hot brand. His jaw hardened as he took in the welt on her cheek, the blood on her lip.

"I'm not afraid of Bobby Gold. Is he the one who hit you?"

Damn the man! He was going to ruin everything. All she needed was for Bobby to find her with a professional card shark—then he'd never believe she'd simply been doing her job honestly.

"I don't care if you're afraid of him or not! I can handle myself, and I want you gone before he finds you here!"

"Did he hit you?" Jack demanded.

Angry heat flowed through her. He simply didn't get it. "That's none of your business. Now go away."

"I can't do that, Cara," he said, his expression darker and more ruthless than any she'd ever seen on Bobby's face. It made her shiver and she took a step back instinctively.

"Just go, Jack. I appreciate the concern, but I'll be fine."

"I hardly think so—"

The door opened again, and Cara's heart sank. Two of Bobby's hired goons hulked into the room, followed by the man himself. If Bobby was surprised to find Jack Wolfe, he didn't show it. In fact, he seemed pleased.

"Well, well," he said. "If it isn't Jack Wolfe. You must like our little Cara, hmm?" He reached out and ran a finger down her bare arm. Cara flinched. "She is quite lovely. I can understand why you'd be tempted."

"You're nothing but scum, Bobby," Jack said. "No matter how hard you try, you'll never be anything more."

Bobby's expression grew positively evil. "I'm sad to say you won't be leaving here with my fifteen million in hand," he said. "It's really too bad you had to cheat. Met the lovely Cara and bribed her to cooperate, did you?"

"Bobby, that's not true!" Cara exclaimed. "I never saw him before tonight—"

Bobby's hand shot out and twisted in her hair. "Shut up," he growled before he slapped her again. The blow stung, but he hadn't cut her this time.

Tears sprang to her eyes, but she wouldn't let them fall. She wouldn't give him the satisfaction.

Bobby shoved her down on the chair. Her hair covered her face and she dragged it back. But not before she heard a scuffle and a punch.

When she could see again, the two bodyguards were holding Jack between them as he jerked hard against them. Blood dripped from one of the guard's noses and Jack's knuckles were scraped.

"You will regret this, Gold," he growled.

"No," Bobby said, his voice full of menace, "you will."

Jack sucked in a torturous breath. His rib cage felt like an elephant had sat on it. He wanted to open his eyes, but it hurt to do so. Where was he? He didn't remember anything beyond the moment when Bobby's thugs had started to beat him. He'd fought back, but two against one were never good odds.

He was in a vehicle now, moving. He had to open his eyes, in spite of the pain, and see if he could figure out where they were going.

It was dark, but he could see the road in front of them and a flash of silver hood in the streetlights. He was sitting in the passenger seat, and the dashboard looked vaguely familiar. The throaty purr of the engine was familiar, as well.

He turned his head on the seat back. Cara

Taylor's profile was the first thing he saw. She looked determined. His gaze followed her arms until he realized her hands were on a steering wheel. She was driving. They were driving. Somewhere.

"How…?" he asked.

Her head whipped sideways, back to the road again. "I told you to leave when you had the chance," she said from between clenched teeth. "I could have fixed it. None of this would have happened."

His laugh was rusty. God, he felt like he'd gotten into a fight with a freight train. "You weren't fixing anything, sweetheart. You cost Gold a lot of money."

It hadn't taken him more than a few moments to realize why she'd been pulled from the game, or why Red Tie had been glaring at her. He was Bobby's ringer, and she had been supposed to make sure he won the pot. That he hadn't figured the truth out sooner, he blamed solely on himself. Perhaps he was as arrogant as the count in his own way. He'd let himself be distracted by lascivious thoughts of Cara. Yes, he'd concentrated on the cards and the reactions of the players, but hadn't let his mind cast wider. If he had, he'd have understood the tension between her and Red Tie sooner.

She glanced at him again. "What makes you think that?"

"Because I know Bobby Gold."

"I figured that," she spat. "You could hardly do what you do without winding up in his casinos from time to time."

Jack shifted, stifling a groan at the sharp pain in his side. "And what is it you think I do?"

She snorted. "You're a gambler, Jack."

He would have laughed if it hadn't hurt so damn much. "How did you get us out of there?"

"Once they knocked you unconscious, Bobby left, but he promised they'd be coming back to finish the job, which I didn't think sounded like an option I wanted to stick around for."

"We're in my car," he said. He recognized the smell, the growl of the engine, the feel of the leather hugging his body.

"I got it from the valet. One of the waiters helped me get you out and put you in the car. I said you were drunk and that I had to drive you home."

He had to hand it to her for thinking of it. Because if they'd stayed in that room, he wasn't too sure that Bobby wouldn't have done a bit more permanent damage.

"And where are we going now?"

"I need to get you to a hospital. But first I

thought it best we get out of Nice. Bobby knows people."

"I know people, too." Hell, he had his own security firm. One call to them, and Bobby Gold would be singing soprano for the next month.

"As soon as we get to the next town, we'll find a doctor."

Jack winced again. "I don't need a doctor. My ribs are bruised, not broken."

"How do you know that?"

"Trust me. I've seen enough injuries to know what is what." Thanks to his father. He'd rarely received the brunt of William's anger, because he could sense when his father was about to explode like a powder keg, but he'd seen the results of his siblings' beatings enough to know which injuries required a visit to the hospital.

"Fine, you don't have broken ribs. But you could have a concussion."

"Doubt it. But if I do, the cure for that is pain-killers and rest."

Cara let out a long-suffering sigh. "Is there anything you don't know, Jack Wolfe?"

"I'm sure there are one or two things."

She didn't laugh. "If you'd just stayed out of it! I could have talked Bobby into forgiving me, could have kept my job and made everything right again."

"You are incredibly naive, Cara. You cost the

man fifteen million euros. Do you really believe he would forget that?"

Her fingers tightened on the wheel. "Once I explained—"

"Explained what? That you aren't a cheat?"

"Yes," she said tightly. "Because I'm not. It's no good now, though, because he believes I planned this with you. Especially since I've helped you get away."

"Why were you working for a man like Gold, anyway?"

She snorted. "Are you telling me that I should have been a card shark instead?"

"Not at all. But you have a talent for numbers, Cara. Surely there are other things you could do."

"Like what?"

"You could find a job in finance—"

"I don't have a college degree. Besides, who are you to talk? Why did you decide to become a gambler?"

He figured he should disabuse her of the notion—but it was far too much fun to let her think he was a professional gambler. He was accustomed to women fawning over him for his money, his family name and his face. To have one angry with him because she believed he was an unscrupulous gambler? It was novel.

"Because I like taking chances." It was true

enough. He got a rush out of playing stocks. Sometimes he didn't sleep for days as he moved between the international markets. Making money was easy. It made sense, unlike everything else in his life. He could control money. He couldn't control the things that had happened to him, or the emotional scars his family bore.

"Well, I don't," she said. "I liked dealing cards. There's no risk in it for me."

"Apparently, there is."

Her jaw tightened. "Tonight was a first."

"It would not have been the last, should you have complied."

She glanced at the gauges. "We're going to need gas soon and I don't have any money."

So she didn't want to admit she'd been in over her head. Fine. "I'll take care of it."

She was silent for a few moments. "Were you playing for someone tonight?"

"No."

"Then you lost a lot of money by coming to look for me. You must regret that impulse."

"It's only money."

She laughed, but it wasn't a humorous sound. "Of course. Because there's no one depending on you for the food on their table or the roof over their head, I suppose."

His employees would no doubt disagree with

that statement. "No, because people are more important than money. You were in trouble."

"I really didn't need rescuing, Jack. You gave up fifteen million for nothing."

"If you weren't in trouble, why are we speeding out of town?"

Before she could acknowledge the truth of that statement, they hit a bump and Jack groaned. Dear God, it felt like there was an alien trying to burst out of his abdomen.

"We need to get you to a doctor," she said worriedly.

Jack swallowed the pain. "No. Because Gold probably *is* looking for us, and it would take too long for my men to arrive. Keep driving."

Bobby Gold had the fifteen mil, but he was the kind of man who couldn't stand to be made a fool of. He'd want Cara Taylor back so he could make her pay for her disobedience. Getting as far from Nice as possible wasn't a bad idea.

Since there were no flights this late, and his private plane was in a hangar in London, they had no choice but to drive. Even if he called his pilot, it would be several hours yet before the plane would arrive.

He'd originally planned a leisurely drive across France on his way to Nathaniel's wedding, anyway. He could have flown, but he knew he needed the time to think. This would be the first time in nearly twenty years that all the Wolfes would be gathered under the same roof—and he wasn't sure how he felt about that. He especially wasn't sure how he felt about seeing Jacob again.

Jacob, who'd betrayed them all when he'd left them without any explanation. Jack had looked up to Jacob, admired him—until the night Jacob had abandoned them.

"You're in no shape to spend the night in a car," Cara said. "A hospital—"

"Just do it," Jack ordered.

He expected an argument, but she flexed her hands on the steering wheel and didn't say anything for several seconds.

"Fine. Where do you want to go?"

Not where he wanted to go. Where he had to go. "England."

CHAPTER THREE

IT WAS nearly two in the morning when they reached the outskirts of Lyon. Cara found a hotel off the expressway and pulled the car into a parking slot. It had taken her a few minutes back in Nice to figure out how to drive Jack's sports car, but once she had, the silver beast was a dream. She knew without asking that it was the most expensive car she'd ever been in, much less driven.

Jack dozed in the passenger seat and she took a moment to study him. Bobby's thugs had beaten him up pretty badly, though they'd hardly touched his face. If he hadn't groaned from time to time, she'd have thought he felt perfectly fine. As it was, she had no idea how badly he was hurt. He said he was only bruised, but she wasn't certain. And it was that uncertainty that had kept her behind the wheel for the past four hours. The farther they got from Bobby, the better.

And then she could talk Jack into going to a hospital.

The skin under his left eye was purpling, but even bruised, he was still devastatingly handsome.

Her pulse kicked up, and she chided herself for reacting to him. Jack Wolfe might be pretty to look at, but he was arrogant and irresponsible—and she had no time for men like that in her life, no matter how his flirtation earlier had made her want to melt in his arms.

She was here because it had seemed the best course to keep driving—especially since he'd been in no shape to do so—but now that they'd arrived in Lyon, she was determined to part ways with the enigmatic Jack Wolfe. Once she got him to a doctor, of course.

The thought of leaving discomfited her, but she shoved it down deep. Why on earth should she care if she ever saw this man again?

"Jack," she said softly.

Surprisingly, he came instantly awake. "Where are we?"

"Lyon. I'm too tired to keep driving. I thought we could get a couple of rooms for the night. If you can loan me the money, I'll pay you back as soon as I can."

It was disconcerting to be here without her purse or passport, but those things had been left behind in the casino when they'd fled. She simply hadn't had time to retrieve them.

"One room," he said.

"I said I'd pay you back."

"It's safer. If Bobby really is looking for us, it's better to be together."

As much as she wanted to, she couldn't argue with that logic. But when she went inside to make the arrangements, she asked for a twin-bedded room. The clerk gave her a key and she returned to fetch Jack. He was taller than she was, and far heavier, but somehow they managed to make it to the room with him leaning against her for support.

The contact sizzled into her. She was conscious of his raw heat, conscious of every single inch of his body where it touched hers. He made her heart pound with his nearness.

"Sorry," he said, his mouth against her hair as he leaned into her while she fitted the key to the door. "You smell delicious," he added.

"Thanks, but compliments will get you nowhere."

"Sweetheart, you have nothing to worry about, I assure you. As much as I might like to have sex with you tonight, I believe the contact would kill me."

The word *sex*, said with that wonderful accent of his, caressed across her senses and lit a flame inside her belly.

Cara swung the door open. There was only one

bed. She hesitated. She could go back down to the clerk and tell him he'd made a mistake, but then she'd have to leave Jack here before returning and helping him to another room. But she couldn't do that to him, not when he was like this.

With a sigh, she guided him over to the bed and sat him down on it. It wasn't a very big bed. She would simply have to sleep on the floor.

"A hot bath would probably do you good," she said, frowning at him as he winced.

One corner of his mouth crooked in a grin. "Do you plan to help me wash, then?"

The heat of a blush rippled over her skin. *Oh, yes.* "No."

"Too bad."

"I'll run the bath for you."

His expression was a mixture of devilishness and gravity. "I'm not going to be able to get into it without help."

Cara's insides went hot and liquid all at once. She hadn't thought of that, but of course he was right. She wanted to refuse, and yet she couldn't. If it would help him to feel better at all, she had to get him into the tub.

"Fine."

He'd already loosened his bow tie earlier and undid the first few studs of his shirt. Cara resolutely slipped the jacket from his shoulders, her heart thudding at his nearness and heat. She had to stand so close to him, her thighs touching his as she stood between his legs. She was conscious of the deep V of her blouse, conscious of his eyes on the slope of her breast. Her skin tingled, her insides tightening.

"You really do smell wonderful," he said.

"It's just soap." She felt self-conscious standing so close to him, felt as if her skin was too tight, as if she would splinter apart if she let this be anything more than a routine task she had to perform.

"Wonderful soap."

"You're a smooth talker, Jack Wolfe," she said as she undid his studs. "But I've heard it all, believe me."

She pulled his shirttails from his trousers. Slipping the shirt off, she tried not to react to the sight of his bare shoulders. They were muscled, not too much, but lean and hard and strong. It shouldn't surprise her that he had the body of an athlete, but it was a bit disconcerting to find that what was underneath the clothes was every bit as enticing as the man in the tuxedo had been.

Focus, Cara.

Pulling the undershirt from his waistband, she lifted it very carefully over his head. Cara had to bite her lip at the broad expanse of bare, toned chest. He was tanned, with the kind of defined pecs and abs that made her giddy—but there was some light bruising over his rib cage where Bobby's thugs had hit him. It would darken over the next few days.

"If I felt better, I might take the way you're looking at me as an invitation."

Cara's gaze snapped up. "Don't flatter yourself. I was looking at your bruises," she said, though she imagined the blush blooming across her cheeks gave away the lie.

He looked down. "It could be worse."

Her chest felt tight. He'd gotten those bruises because of her. Because he'd gone after Bobby when Bobby had hit her. Even if it had been unnecessary, even if she hadn't needed his help, she had to acknowledge that he'd gotten hurt because he'd tried to help. It made her angry and sad at the same time.

"I don't see how it could be worse."

"Trust me, it could."

"Are you accustomed to getting beaten up, then?" She was trying to inject a bit of humor into the conversation, but his expression said that she'd failed miserably. His jaw looked as if it had been carved out of granite. His eyes were flat, bleak. She sensed she'd stumbled into quicksand. "Don't answer that—"

He lifted a hand, traced his fingers over her bottom lip. Her heart raced like the powerful engine in his car, but she didn't move to stop him.

She couldn't. His touch felt too good, too raw and honest.

"Are you afraid for me, Cara? Afraid of what I might tell you?"

"I—" She didn't know what to say. Her heart was a painful knot in her chest. She sensed they'd crossed some sort of demarcation line, that there would be no going back now. Ever. "I should run the bath," she blurted.

Because standing here while this man touched her wasn't the best idea she'd ever had. He evoked sensations she'd never experienced, sensations she wanted desperately to explore. But he was all wrong for her. *This* was wrong.

He was a gambler, a card shark—he wasn't the sort of man a girl could rely on. And she didn't need a man in her life, anyway. It never turned out well. She needed to go, needed to run the bath— and she needed to get away from him as soon as possible, before her silly heart decided she liked his touch, his attention. Before she decided she wanted more.

"Does it hurt?" he asked, his fingers ghosting over the split in her lip.

"A little."

"Was this the first time?"

It took her a moment to figure out what he meant. "Bobby never hit me before, no. I didn't like him much, but the pay was good and the bonus he promised to those of us who came to Nice was even better."

"But you didn't get the money."

Cara sighed. "No. I don't suppose I ever will now."

Mama and Remy would be fine, though. Cara would find another job and keep sending money home just like always. And Evie was still there, working and helping Mama with Remy. A tiny voice in Cara's head asked when she would get to do what she wanted in life—but she shoved it aside angrily. She would do what needed to be done. Always. Daddy might have abandoned the family, but Cara never would.

She stepped back, out of Jack's reach. His hand dropped. He looked like a beautiful dark angel, his torso bare and bruised. He was delicious, tempting, and she was appalled that she thought so. Appalled that if he weren't hurt, she could picture herself pushing him back against the pillows, her mouth on his, their limbs tangling. She could picture the moment when he entered her body, the way she would shudder beneath him, her body rippling in one long, ecstatic wave.

"You're a cruel woman, Cara Taylor," Jack said, pulling her from her tangled thoughts.

"How can that possibly be?" she said softly. "I'm helping you, aren't I? I could have left you for Bobby to finish off."

"I almost wish you had. It would be easier than watching you look at me like I'm an ice cream cone. Do you want to lick me, Cara?"

Oh, God.

There was nothing to do but brazen it out. "You're very handsome," she said as coolly as she could, "but you already know that. I can enjoy the view, but that doesn't mean I want to do anything about it."

His laugh was raspy. "I'd like to enjoy the view, as well. How about you take some things off for me? Doesn't seem fair you get to ogle and I don't."

If she turned any redder, she'd burst into flame. "No one ever said life was fair."

The heat and humor in his eyes banked for a moment. For some reason, it bothered her. He was mercurial, Jack Wolfe. She wanted to know what he was thinking, what kind of memories had the power to dim the heat in those remarkable eyes. The thought it might be a woman did not comfort her.

No, it made her prickly. And that made no sense at all.

"Why don't you go run that bath?" he finally said when they'd been staring at each other for several moments without speaking.

She felt like she should say something, but instead she went into the bathroom and turned on the tap. What was wrong with her? Why couldn't she manage to string two coherent sentences together when he looked at her as if he wanted to devour her? She'd fielded plenty of come-ons from drunken gamblers during her time working in the casino—she knew what to say, how to deflate their ambition while also keeping them at the table. So why couldn't she find that skill with this man?

When she returned to the bedroom, Jack had managed to stand on his own. He'd undone his belt and zipper, but his pants hung low on his hips, revealing smooth skin and a dark arrow of hair pointing the way to his groin. Cara swallowed as her heart picked up speed again.

God, she was acting like a timid virgin. She had to stop this nonsense, had to help him into the tub before she could lie on the bed and turn on the television. It was late, but she was too keyed up to sleep just now. A bit of mindless television was usually just what the doctor ordered when insomnia hit.

"Do you need help?" she asked, praying he would say no. His shirt was one thing, but his pants?

For once, he looked apologetic instead of devilish. "I'm afraid you'll have to take them off. Bending is hell at the moment."

Cara thought of something her friend LeeAnn

had once said. LeeAnn had gone to nursing school and now worked in the ICU, taking care of critical patients. According to LeeAnn, you got used to seeing naked men after a while. It was just a job, no matter how good-looking the man.

Cara squared her shoulders. Yes, this was a job, a mission of mercy. Jack Wolfe was attractive, but this wasn't about attraction. This was about helping a patient into the bath.

Except that, even in this state, he seemed too big, too virile and male, to be a patient. He was stiff and sore, but he wasn't incapacitated.

Determinedly, she pushed his trousers down his hips until all that was left were a pair of boxers.

"I should warn you," he said when she hooked her fingers into the waistband. Cara looked up, met his silver gaze head-on. His eyes were both cool and hot and she wondered how he did that, how he managed to seem so in control and on the edge all at once. "I'm not unaffected by a beautiful woman removing my clothes, even in this state."

Cara licked suddenly dry lips. Her throat felt like sand. Jack's eyes darkened as he followed the movement of her tongue.

"I'll keep it in mind," she managed huskily.

And then she was bending and sliding his boxers down his muscled thighs until she could let them fall at his feet. Resolutely, she focused on his face as she stood again. She would not look down, would not look at that part of him she was suddenly dying to see.

"Seeing down your shirt just now didn't help," he added. "In case you were wondering."

"You're not in any shape to flirt with me," she said firmly, "so you really should stop."

"Can't help it."

Nor could she help it when her gaze dropped, in spite of her resolution not to look. Cara's breath caught, held, until she felt dizzy from the lack of oxygen. He was beautiful. And he was definitely aroused.

"Like what you see?"

"It doesn't matter," she said. "You're in no shape to do anything about it, as you've already noted."

"I'm not." He lifted an eyebrow in challenge. "But you are."

Cara's ears burned. Not because he shocked her, but because a part of her wanted to do it. She wanted him at her mercy, wanted to tame and control and possess. All she had to do was drop to her knees, take him in her mouth and—

"Forget it. I'm not some kind of good-time girl, Jack Wolfe. We're here because you couldn't leave well enough alone, not because I can't resist your charm."

"Too bad."

"Come on," she said as she slipped an arm around his waist—sweet heaven, his *bare* waist. "Let's get you into the bath. The warm water will help."

Somehow she got him into the bathroom and into the tub, though she got soaked in the process. He stretched out his legs—they were still bent since the tub was shorter than he was—and groaned.

"God this hurts."

Her heart squeezed in sympathy. "I'm sorry, Jack."

"Don't worry. You can make it up to me later."

Later. As if she would still be here. Cara shook her head. No, she wasn't staying. She wasn't succumbing to the need to be near this man.

Need? Was it already that bad?

No. Because she'd let herself be fooled once—at least for a short time—by her feelings for James, and she knew better now. She didn't need a man. She liked men, enjoyed good sex, but she didn't *need* a man. And definitely not *this* man.

"You never quit, do you?" she said, grabbing a towel so she could go into the bedroom and remove her wet clothes.

"Sweetheart, if I were dead I'd still want to have sex with you."

"Charming." But her pulse was pounding, fluttering. "I'll be in the other room. Yell if you need me."

Cara changed out of her wet clothes and hung them on a chair to dry. Then she wrapped the towel around her body and climbed onto the bed, scooting back against the pillows as she turned on the television. But instead of finding anything she wanted to watch, her gaze kept straying to Jack's cell phone on the bedside table.

It was early evening in Louisiana...

"Jack?"

"Yes?"

She picked up the phone and went to the bathroom door. "Can I make a call to the States on your phone? I'll pay you."

He didn't even look at her. His head was tilted back, his eyes closed. He lifted two fingers where they rested on the edge of the tub. "Go ahead."

"Thanks." She turned away, then stopped. "Do you need anything?"

"Nothing you're willing to provide," he said on a long drawl.

She shook her head as she went back to the bed and climbed onto it. Twenty seconds later, Mama's voice came on the other end of the line. A flood of wistfulness washed over Cara. Oddly enough, tears pricked her. She pressed her eyelids to keep them from falling.

"Hey, Mama."

The conversation didn't last long, but it helped her feel better in the end. Remy was doing well. The money Cara had sent recently would pay for his therapy through the end of next month. Evie had just gotten a job as a secretary in a law firm downtown, and the insurance was paid up for the next two months. The ground beneath her family's feet was firm, if not quite solid yet.

When the call ended, she laid the phone on the table and closed her eyes. They were doing well. Not great, but well. She could have used the money that Bobby had been about to pay her, but it wasn't the end of the world. Besides, that had been dirty money, and Mama wouldn't have approved of dirty money. Cara would just have to find a new job, work harder and make damn sure her family stayed on firmer ground.

She roused herself and went to check on Jack. He looked up when she came in. The skin under his eye looked worse, but there was no swelling.

"How do you feel?" she asked.

"Stiff. I'm ready to get out of here."

He pushed himself upright until she could get an arm around him and help him to stand. Grabbing a towel, she wrapped it around him, then handed him another one to dry his torso with. The towel she wore kept slipping as they walked toward the bed. She prayed it would hold until she got him into bed when she could tighten it again.

"Why are you still here?" Jack asked.

The question startled her. "Because you're too stubborn to go to a doctor."

"If I did, would you leave?"

She hesitated only a moment. "Yes," she said, though the word wanted to stick in her throat.

"A good reason not to go, then."

"Jack—"

"But where would you go?" he interrupted. "Where is home?"

He lay on the bed and she pulled the covers up. "New Orleans," she told him.

"A grand city."

"You've been to the casino there, no doubt," she said a bit crisply.

"I have. But why aren't you working there? It's far safer than working for a man like Bobby Gold."

Cara shrugged. She didn't want him to know the truth. That she felt like she'd never make anything of herself if she stayed in Louisiana, that she wanted adventure and romance, and that she wanted to travel to far-flung places. It sounded childish when she said it. And yet those were the longings of her heart. She wanted to escape. She'd always wanted to escape.

Guilt stabbed into her. She had no right to feel that way.

"I thought there was more money to be made in

Vegas." She picked up a pillow and clutched it to her chest. "Why don't you go to sleep now? It'll do you good."

He tipped his head at the pillow. "Planning to suffocate me in my sleep?"

"It's a thought," she said. "But no. I'm going to sleep on the floor."

He caught her wrist in a broad hand before she could turn away. "There's no need for that, Cara. It'll be uncomfortable."

"I'll be fine."

"This bed is big enough for two."

She wasn't sure this *room* was big enough for two when he was the other person sharing it with her. He encroached on her space simply by breathing. Made her jumpy and achy all at once.

"I'd hate to bump into your ribs in the night," she said. The words were hardly more than a whisper.

"I appreciate your concern. But I don't think that's the reason."

"Of course it is," she said.

"Get in the bed, Cara. You can put the pillow between us if it makes you feel better. To protect my ribs," he added.

Was that sarcasm she heard in his voice?

But she was tempted. Because the floor would be hard, and because she was so tired and achy already that she just wanted to sleep in a soft bed.

Tomorrow, everything would look better, especially if she slept well. Her head would be clear and she could think of what to do next. Of how to get home when her passport and all her money was back in Nice.

"Fine," she said. "But if you touch me anywhere inappropriate, I'll black your other eye."

Jack only laughed.

CHAPTER FOUR

JACK slept fitfully. The injuries woke him from time to time, but it was the proximity of the warm woman next to him and the dreams he sunk into whenever he fell asleep that kept bringing him back to the surface. He wanted to reach for her, pull her into the curve of his body and just hold her. Because he wanted to be close to someone.

The dreams hadn't bothered him in years, but tonight they were back in force. His father was a chameleon, making them all laugh and building a fabulous tree house for them one moment, only to explode the next. The screaming and rage rained down on him, on his brothers and sister, like fire from above. The tree house was destroyed as the sobs of his younger siblings rent the air.

But Jack had never cried when his father raged.

Unlike the others, he'd always known when William was on the verge of cracking and he'd mostly avoided his father's wrath. But he'd ached for his siblings, for the ones who seemed to draw William's attention most of all. Tonight, it seemed as if he was destined to relive those memories every time he closed his eyes.

And he figured he knew why. Nathaniel's wedding...the trip home. In a couple of days, he would probably come face-to-face with Jacob again. Jacob, who he'd looked up to and admired. Who he'd wanted to be exactly like when he was growing up.

Until Jacob had betrayed them. Until he'd left and they'd had to learn how to live without him there to guide them. He'd loved Jacob, but Jacob hadn't loved him—them—enough to stay.

Though it hurt like hell, he pushed himself up and swung his legs from the bed. If one of Bobby's men hadn't delivered a blow that had knocked him unconscious, he'd hate to think of the sort of shape he'd be in now. Because they would have kept punching until they did more damage than just a few bruised ribs.

"What are you doing?" Cara cried, scrambling up beside him.

"Looking for something to drink."

"I'll get it. You stay there."

He hated being dependent, hated that she'd had to help him undress when it wasn't for pleasure. But he let her get up and go to the minifridge. When she bent down and opened it up, the interior light shone on her bare legs, on the curves of her bottom beneath the towel she still wore. His body reacted, in spite of the aches and pains.

"There's water, juice, soda—"

"Water's fine."

She twisted off the cap and brought the bottle to him. He took it and drank, his eyes skimming her lush body in the meager light peeking between the closed curtains.

"How do you feel now?" she asked.

"Like I've been run over by a train."

"I need to leave," she blurted. "My passport and money are still in Nice, and I can't go home without them."

Something inside him twisted at the thought of her leaving. "It's too dangerous, Cara. You need to stay away from Gold."

Her golden-green eyes sparked with temper. "Maybe you didn't hear me, but I can't leave Europe without my passport. What am I supposed to do, hide from Bobby forever? If I take some friends with me, he won't bother me."

Jack couldn't help but laugh, though it hurt to do so. "Stay away from Nice, and stay away from Bobby."

She crossed her arms beneath her breasts. Did she realize, he wondered, that the towel inched up and revealed a hint of what lay beneath? His body turned to stone. He didn't even care that it hurt.

"I'm not your property, Jack. You can't tell me what to do."

God but she exasperated him. Was she that obtuse or did she just delight in contradicting him? "I'm trying to protect you."

If anything, that statement only made her angrier. "Protect me? My God, if you hadn't come barreling in like the Lone Ranger, it'd all be over with and I'd be on my way home again. I don't *need* your help, Jack. In fact, I'd be better off without it!"

Anger flashed through him. He'd taken a bloody beating for her, and she still insisted she'd have been fine. "Right. Because when Bobby's boys needed a punching bag, they'd have just had to do without because you're a woman."

"God!" She shoved both hands through her hair, whipping it off her shoulders and then letting it fall again, a silken waterfall down her back. "They hit you because you hit *them*. I've never seen Bobby abuse any of the girls. He was angry with me and he slapped me. But that's the extent of it. Or would have been if you hadn't shown up."

Jack reached for the watch he'd left on the bedside table—9:00 a.m. He was done arguing with her because it was pointless. She was determined to do her own thing—and maybe she was right.

Maybe Bobby's anger would have faded a bit since he'd gotten the jackpot after all.

Some people were determined to keep flying into the fire, even when they knew they would get singed. Jack knew better, had always known better. And he had little patience with those who did not.

"Fine, then. You go back to Nice. I'm going to London."

She didn't think he would be able to do it, but Jack managed to dress on his own. Then he made a call on his mobile. She heard him ask for a Dr. Drake, so at least he was finally planning to get checked out. The knowledge relieved her, made her not worry quite so much about what he would do when she was gone.

Twenty minutes later, there was a knock on the door. He opened it and took a package from a young man wearing jeans and a faded rock band T-shirt.

Cara ran the towel over her freshly washed hair as she watched him open the package and take out a couple of bottles. She'd put her clothes back on, though they were still slightly damp. It was uncomfortable, but that couldn't be helped. She had to leave, and she had nothing else to wear.

Except she had no cash to go anywhere. How would she get back to Nice when she had no money, no credit cards and no ATM card? She had to ask Jack for money, and that galled her. She already owed him for the night in the hotel, and the phone call, and she hated that she had to ask for yet another loan. She was used to paying her own way, to taking care of herself, and to be dependent on this man she hardly knew for money to eat and sleep—and get back to Nice—bothered her more than she could say. She felt wrong asking, and yet she had no choice.

She *would* pay him back. Even if he didn't believe it.

Jack took a couple of pills from the bottles and washed them down with water. Cara blinked. What kind of man could call a doctor and have painkillers delivered twenty minutes later? It forced her to reevaluate her assessment of him. He might be a gambler, but he was obviously a very good one. Perhaps he came from money and never really had to worry about what would happen if he lost everything.

Wouldn't that be nice? Cara thought wistfully.

He looked up, met her gaze. His expression didn't soften from the hard mask he'd donned when she'd told him she was leaving. Her heart flipped in response. She had to stifle an urge to go to him, to run her fingers through his hair, to caress his granite jaw and press her lips to his.

He slipped a wallet from the tuxedo jacket

he'd left lying on the bed. Then he took out some euro notes and tossed them on the bed. "You'll be needing that," he said.

Perversely, her eyes filled with tears. Angry tears, tears of frustration. She'd been worried about asking for cash, and he'd preempted her. She wanted to tell him to keep his damn money, and yet she couldn't. Without it, she'd be standing on a Lyon street by nightfall, singing *a cappella* and hoping she could earn enough coins to eat dinner.

"Thank you," she said instead, shame a living creature inside her belly. It roiled and twisted until she wanted to lock herself in the bathroom and heave into the toilet.

"Take care of yourself, Cara." He watched her for a long moment, as if he wanted to say something else—or maybe he was waiting for her to say something—before he turned and walked out the door. He didn't walk with the fluid grace that he had when she'd first seen him, but he still moved like a man in control of his life and destiny.

She heard the roar of the engine start after what seemed like forever. And then the tires were squealing out of the parking lot and she was alone.

Cara let out the breath she'd been holding. He'd left her. Oddly, it hurt that he had.

But she'd *told* him to go! Cara pressed her

fingers to her temples and sucked in a sharp breath. What was wrong with her? She'd wanted him gone, wanted to be on her own again so she could think and plan and breathe without Jack Wolfe taking up all the oxygen in the room.

She clutched the bills in her hand, only now realizing that she'd not gotten his address or phone number so she could pay him back. He'd given her five hundred euros, and now she felt as if she'd opened his wallet and taken them herself. Because she had no way to ever repay him.

But is that really the problem, Cara?

It wasn't, and she knew it. She could track him down again, no matter how difficult the task. But the real problem was that Jack Wolfe had sparked something inside her, something she'd never quite felt before. She didn't know why that was—he was too arrogant, too entitled, too much of a good-time guy who worked the casino racket and made a living off the cards. He wasn't the kind of man she liked at all.

But the physical attraction to him had been off the charts. As if that were a reason to feel so forlorn that she'd never see him again.

Cara took one last look at the room. It was time to go, time to get a taxi to the train station. She didn't have the luxury to remember Jack's nude body, his raw male beauty and power. She only need step through the door and close it behind her and Jack Wolfe would be a memory.

Resolutely, she did just that. The hotel reminded her a bit of one of those cheap chain motels in the States, an industrial box of a building close to the autoroute. She looked at the traffic moving on the highway and imagined Jack was several miles away by now. He wasn't thinking of her anymore. He was thinking of home and how long it would take him to get there.

She hoped he would be okay, that he wouldn't push himself too hard when he was still recovering. Maybe she should have gone along with him, if only to drive him to his destination. What would another day or two matter? Perhaps Bobby's temper would have cooled even more by then.

Cara walked toward the front office. Jack was gone and that was the end of it. She would ask the desk clerk to call a taxi for her and then she, too, would be on her way.

Before she reached the office, however, a familiar engine revved and she turned as Jack whipped into the parking lot and stopped beside her. Ridiculously, her heart leaped into her throat. Why was she so happy to see him?

"I have an idea," he said, that delightful accent rolling over her, making her shiver.

"I'm listening," she replied, keeping her voice as cool as possible in spite of her pounding pulse.

"I have to go to a wedding in a couple of days and I need a date."

Cara frowned. "You want me to be your date?"

"I'll pay you. And I'll make sure you get your passport and bank cards back."

She was conscious of the cash he'd given her burning a hole in her pocket. "But why would you want to pay me to go to a wedding with you?"

He raked a hand through his dark hair. He looked tousled, sexy, and she found herself wanting to repeat the motion with her own fingers. No way on earth did this man need to pay for a date.

"You need a job, I need a date. Seems the perfect solution."

She stiffened as her throat felt suddenly tight with emotion. He thought she was the kind of woman who needed money so badly that she would do anything to get it. "I'm sure you know plenty of willing partners who don't need to be paid."

She felt cheap, dirty, disappointed in a way she hadn't when he'd given her the five hundred euros to get home. Now he was offering to pay her, as if she were a professional escort. It hurt.

She took the money from her pocket and thrust it at him. "I'm not for sale, Jack. I told you that before."

Jack groaned. "Cara, for God's sake, I'm trying

to help you. Whatever bonus Bobby was planning to give you, I'll double it."

"How can you say that? You have no idea how much—"

"So tell me."

"Twenty-five thousand," she ground out, certain he would laugh in her face at the sum.

He shrugged. "Fine, we'll make it fifty, then. What do you say?"

Cara's lungs refused to work. He couldn't be serious. And yet—

My God, she'd be able to take care of *everything,* be able to pay off the remaining debt on the house, pay the insurance premiums and make sure that Mama never had to worry again. Remy could get the extra therapy he needed without Mama sacrificing so much to do it. Evie could have a normal life.

Did it really matter if her pride stung or if it made her feel cheap that Jack had offered to pay her to be his date? She'd been willing to throw a card game for money, even if she hadn't actually done so, so why couldn't she be Jack's date?

It was much less onerous than cheating, after all. But still…

"Don't be stupid, Cara," Jack said. "This is a far better deal than working for Bobby Gold."

Oh, God, was she really thinking about it? She was. The fact her feet were glued to the spot and she hadn't yet spun on her heel and walked away told her she was.

But it was more than the money. So much more.

She hadn't spent much time with Jack, but she'd spent enough to know that she was wildly attracted to him. More than that, she could trust him to deliver on his promise. He wouldn't leave her in the lurch the way James had. He'd live up to his end of the bargain.

All she had to do was go to a wedding. How hard was that?

She *had* to do it, regardless of the pinprick to her feelings.

"I know you don't think so," Jack continued, "but I'm not convinced Bobby won't hurt you if you go back. He's a small man, Cara, and he holds grudges. You crossed him—"

"Yes," she blurted before she could talk herself out of it.

Jack blinked. "You'll do it?"

Oh, God.

"Yes, I'll be your date." She went around and climbed into the passenger seat of the shiny silver beast. Her heart pounded with adrenaline and recklessness. "But don't you get any other ideas, Jack Wolfe," she said once she was belted in. "You've bought a date, not a bed partner."

Jack caught her hand and lifted it to his lips.

The touch of his mouth against the tender inside skin of her wrist sent a shiver prickling over her "I know that. Because when you *do* come to my bed, it won't be because I've paid you to do so."

"Someone needs to prove to you that you aren' irresistible," she forced out, though her body was already beginning to sing from that single touch Belatedly, as if just remembering, she yanked her hand from his grip.

"Maybe," he said with a grin. "But I'm hoping it's not you."

The kilometers ticked by in silence. Jack glanced over at Cara on occasion, but she seemed as los in thought as he was. He'd been about to make the turn onto the autoroute when he'd realized he had to go back for her. She was stubborn and de termined to be independent, and though he un derstood that, he couldn't allow her to return to Nice. Because there was no doubt in his mind tha Bobby Gold would hurt her.

He didn't know Cara Taylor's story, but he wanted to. And, selfishly, he wanted to avoid any confrontations with Jacob or Lucas at Nathaniel': wedding. He'd almost decided not to go to the wedding, simply to avoid the unpleasantness o any conversations with his two older brothers, bu it would hurt Nathaniel if he didn't show up.

Having Cara with him seemed a perfect solu

tion. With a beautiful woman by his side, his brothers wouldn't dare try and talk to him about things he had no interest in discussing.

What was there left to say?

He was still angry, still bitter. He knew it.

Jack's fingers tightened on the wheel. He didn't want to do this, didn't want to think about those dark years when everything had fallen apart. He'd once been so close to his older brothers, especially Jacob…and now there was nothing. Nothing but an empty void.

"Do you want me to drive?"

Jack glanced at Cara. Her long dark hair had dried in a tousled mess of spiral curls. It made her look so sexy and touchable when combined with the low-cut shirt and tight satin mini. He wanted to pull the car over to the side of the road and tug her onto his lap. Golden-green eyes gazed back at him coolly—but there was a hint of fire she couldn't quite hide. It gratified him, buoyed him. This attraction between them was mutual—and he knew they would act on it soon enough, even if she didn't. It was inevitable.

"I've got it for now," he said.

"You seem tense. I thought maybe your ribs were hurting."

Jack rolled his shoulders. He was tense, but not because he hurt. "They hurt, yes, but not too badly I can't drive awhile longer."

"Just let me know when you need me to take over, okay?"

"We won't go much farther. I have an apartment in Paris. We'll stop there for the night. Besides, we need to go shopping."

She folded her arms over her breasts in a self-conscious gesture. He wondered what had happened to the bow tie. She seemed to have lost it somewhere along the way.

"I'm sorry I'm not better prepared," she said.

"How could you be?"

She turned to him again, her face both serious and eager at once. "I don't dress like this all the time," she said. "I do have decent clothing."

"I never doubted it."

She waved a hand over her body. "This isn't even my usual uniform. Bobby said it was something special for the game, something to keep the men playing for high stakes."

"It certainly worked for me," he told her. "I kept hoping to get a glimpse every time you bent over."

Her face reddened—and then she laughed. "You lost fifteen million euros because you wanted to see down my shirt? Wow, and here I thought a guy like you could get a woman naked whenever he wanted."

"Can I get you naked?"

"No."

"But you've seen me. I think I deserve a turn."

The blush on her creamy skin was intriguing. She crossed her legs, those impossibly long sexy legs, and he grew instantly hard. She wanted him, no matter how she tried to pretend otherwise. He knew enough about women to know that—even if Cara Taylor was proving surprisingly difficult to read for the most part.

"This is business, Jack. Don't forget it. And whatever clothes you buy for me, please take them out of the money you're planning to pay me."

"Fine, if that's what you want." Jack shook his head. She was unlike any of the women he'd ever dated. Most women would leap at the chance to have a designer wardrobe added to the pot, but not Cara.

"It is."

"So why were you working for Gold in the first place?" He was truly curious about how a sweet girl like her ended up with a shark like Gold.

She sighed and turned her head on the seat. In the distance, villages perched in the center of rolling vineyards. Fields of sunflowers blazoned against the landscape at regular intervals. It was beautiful and peaceful, and he suddenly wished he could just keep driving, just the two of them in the car alone, talking and watching the scenery flow by.

"You may have heard of Hurricane Katrina," she said.

"Yes."

"My mama lost her house in the flood. It took months to clear the land and rebuild everything. In the meanwhile, we lived in a trailer provided by the government. It was tiny, cramped."

She hesitated for a few moments, and he wondered if she would continue. Then she cleared her throat.

"There were some things that happened, things that Mama wasn't expecting, but we finally got the house rebuilt enough to live in. Then I went to Vegas," she said, shrugging. "It seemed like the thing to do at the time. I was seeing someone, and he lost his job. He said we could make a lot more in Vegas, because tourism was strong, and I definitely needed extra money to help out at home. Tourism had dried up in New Orleans, you see…" She took a breath, turned to look at him, almost as if she were daring him to say anything negative about her choices. "I waitressed for a while, but when one of the casinos announced they needed dealer trainees, I applied. The money was supposed to be better, and I wanted to send more home."

She shrugged again, as if it meant nothing— and yet he was certain it meant everything. "I worked for someone else for a while, but Bobby offered me more money. So I took it."

Jack's grip tightened on the wheel instinctively. He understood the drive to help family only too well. The need, the desperation, the necessity. They were more alike than she knew.

"So what happened to the boyfriend?"

Her fingers clenched in her lap. "We parted ways." She turned to him, fixed him with the full force of her wounded stare. He didn't think she could possibly be aware of all she revealed in that look. "He stole my money and ran off with an exotic dancer."

Jack wanted to grind his teeth. But he said, "Then he wasn't very bright, was he?"

She gave a little laugh. "You're too nice. But you don't really know me. Maybe the dancer was a better choice. Maybe I'm horrible or something."

It was his turn to laugh. "Not a chance, Cara."

"How do you know?" she challenged.

He glanced at her before concentrating on the road again. "Because you didn't leave me at Bobby's mercy. Because you sacrificed your job for me."

"I didn't do it for you," she interjected. "At least, not the job part."

"No, you couldn't cheat because it's not who you are. But I still feel responsible. Bobby's guy probably would have won without me there. He was the best player, besides me."

"It doesn't matter," she said. "What happened happened. There's no sense crying over it now."

She was strong, this woman. He admired that about her.

"How did you end up in Nice, anyway?"

She leaned back on the seat, her head lolling to one side. "Bobby took only his best employees, and he promised us all a huge bonus. It seemed like a good idea at the time. I've never been to Europe before," she added in a soft voice.

"And is it everything you thought it would be?"

"I really don't know." She sighed, a soft sound that whispered over his senses and made him wonder if she would sigh like that in bed. "I've been working nonstop for the opening, so I never had a chance to explore. Bobby rented an apartment block to house us in and sent a van every day to pick us up. All I saw of Nice was from a car window."

"Didn't you ever have a day off?"

"No. I've only been in France for two weeks, and we worked every day."

"Then maybe you need to do a little sightseeing." The wedding was in two days, so he had plenty of time to get there. Besides, if he were in Paris, there would be no chance that Jacob would track him down before the wedding. "Tonight I'll take you to a great café I know for dinner, and then perhaps a cruise on the Seine."

Her face lit up as she turned to him. "I'd love that. I've always wanted to go to Paris, ever since I read Hemingway's *A Moveable Feast* in high school."

"I like seeing you smile," he said. She dropped her chin, hiding her eyes from him. He wondered what he would see there, wanted very much to see it, but she kept her gaze lowered.

"I'm not sure what I'm doing here," she said after a few moments of silence. "But I like you. I'm learning to trust you, Jack, and I hope you don't disappoint me."

Something squeezed tight inside his chest. Because he always disappointed the women in his life. He meant well, but he inevitably got bored. Once he'd played anything long enough—cards, stocks, women—it was time to move on to the next challenge. He wasn't stupid enough to think he hadn't left broken hearts in his wake. Wasn't stupid enough to think that Cara was different somehow. She had his attention now, but how long would it last?

"I like you, too," he said. And then, because he *did* like her, because he thought she was charming and naive and too trusting, he told her the truth. "But don't trust me, Cara. Don't ever trust me."

CHAPTER FIVE

DON'T trust me.

Cara stood at the window of the room she'd been given in Jack's apartment and stared at the Eiffel Tower in the distance. Below, boats moved along the Seine, and cars zipped down the streets while the sidewalks were crowded with Parisians going about their daily business. It was a beautiful city, so vibrant and alive, and she was giddy with the thought she was actually here.

But the way Jack had told her not to trust him kept popping into her mind like an annoying mosquito. She couldn't make it go away, couldn't forget how he'd said the words—so bleak and raw that it made her soul ache.

She hadn't known what to say then, had been embarrassed she'd said anything at all. It wasn't like her to open up to anyone, and especially not to someone like Jack Wolfe. She hardly knew him, and yet they'd been through so much together—

and he'd seemed so honorable—that she felt she could maybe learn to trust him.

That he'd told her not to had shocked her into speechlessness, and they'd finished the drive in relative silence. At least until they reached Paris and she couldn't keep her awe to herself. Jack had once more become the solicitous, attentive host and he'd pointed out the sights as they drove. She'd gasped and closed her eyes more than once the closer they'd gotten into the center of town, certain that his lovely car was about to crash into another of the crazy drivers who frequented the streets.

But it never happened. Cars passed one another with only a hairbreadth between them, but somehow everyone made it unscathed. Jack had driven up to a grand building on a side street and touched a button in the car. A garage door cranked upward and he zipped the car inside.

It wasn't until they'd entered his apartment that the truth had hit her: Jack Wolfe was extremely wealthy. The apartment was glorious, with high ceilings and original architecture—plaster friezes, ornate moldings and polished wooden floors that gleamed with the richness of age and frequent care.

The furniture was modern—sleek leather couches and chairs—and the views were spectacular. She could see so much of the famous city from the huge floor-to-ceiling windows running the length of the room that it took her breath away.

Jack had shown her to this room to freshen up. In the bathroom, she'd found all the toiletries she could need, a hairbrush, a toothbrush and a fluffy white robe. In spite of her morning shower, she'd taken another, washing her hair and blow-drying it so it hung smooth and sleek down her back.

A knock at the door startled her. Heart pounding, she moved toward the entry.

"Yes?"

"I've had some things sent up for you."

Cara pulled the door open. Jack stood there, so tall and handsome that he took her breath away. His eye was black, but it didn't detract from his male beauty. He looked more relaxed now, and more dangerous.

Jack Wolfe was not the sort of man she needed to get involved with. She no longer believed he was simply a gambler—oh, he was definitely a gambler, but that wasn't the *only* thing he did— but she was certain he was bad for her. He was, she realized, a daredevil. She had little to base it on, other than the way he'd behaved at the card table and later when he'd come looking for her. He'd faced Bobby with contempt, and he'd fought hard against the men who'd punched him, never once begging for mercy.

But she knew she was correct, that she'd surmised the truth.

He thrived on challenge and adrenaline. He got a rush from danger. He was the worst kind of man in the world for any woman, but especially for her. She wanted someone who was dependable, who was stable and responsible. She wanted what she'd never had.

But why was she thinking *any* of these thoughts? She barely knew this man, and she certainly wasn't planning to fall in love with him.

"Can I come in?"

Cara swallowed as she pulled the door wider. Heat blossomed in her belly, between her thighs, crept along her skin in a crimson wave. "Of course."

He passed inside, carrying bags from a boutique, and set them on the antique table at the end of the bed. "It's not much, but it's enough to go out shopping and to dinner."

Embarrassed, she went over and peeked inside one of the bags.

"If you don't like it, I'll have something else sent up. I had to guess at your size."

"I'm sure you did fine," she replied politely.

"Technically, it wasn't me. I simply made a phone call and described you to the shopgirls." His mouth crooked in a smile. A devilish smile. "Aren't you going to look?"

"I am looking."

"No, you're peeking past the tissue. Take them out, see what you think. There's time to send it all back if it's not right."

She withdrew a jewel green sweater set made of the finest tightly knit silk and a pair of cream slacks from one of the bags.

"The color suits you," he said as her heart beat harder. "Matches your eyes."

"Thank you." The sweater set was gorgeous, expensive, and she adored the color. It was the kind of thing she'd have bought for herself, if she'd had the money to do so. Most of her clothes came from big-box stores, huge chains that thrived on quantity not quality. It was what she could afford, and she'd never once felt as if she looked cheap—until now. "Everything is beautiful," she told him with a hard knot in her throat.

"I'm glad you like them."

In the next bag, she found a box with a pair of strappy kitten heels. "The size is absolutely perfect."

"I saw the bottom of your shoe when you had your leg tucked beneath you in the car."

"No wonder we nearly ran into that yellow van," she teased. Because she didn't know what else to do. This moment was so intimate, so private and personal, and she felt out of sorts in a way. He wasn't her lover, yet he'd bought clothes for her.

It's a job, Cara, she reminded herself. There was nothing wrong with what she was doing, being here with him like this. It was different than any job she'd had before, true, but it was still a job. And she had no suitable clothes for the wedding. This was simply part of the process. She tried to ignore the fact she was in a bathrobe, and that she had nothing on underneath.

"Look in the pink bag," he said, eyes glinting silvery hot.

Cara's fingers touched silk. She pulled out a delicate white bra and thong—and shoved them back inside again as Jack laughed. She was so far in over her head that it wasn't funny. Had she really thought she was going to keep this about business between them?

"So modest. I like that about you," he said.

Cara straightened her spine as she stared at him. It was hard to be quelling when you were in a bathrobe. "I'm not in the habit of showing my underwear to men I hardly know. It's not polite."

He laughed again as he took a step toward her. "Can you really say we hardly know each other after last night?"

Heat enveloped her, wrapped her in its web, made her long for another look at his naked body. She'd tried not to look, but she hadn't succeeded. And she couldn't forget what she'd seen. The long, strong legs. The lean hips, the jutting sex. The flat

abdomen and muscled torso. He'd had a tan line
she remembered, a boundary line where she could
run her tongue and see if it drove him as insane as
she imagined it would.

Stop.

"Once again, Cara, there's an invitation in your
eyes."

"You think too highly of yourself—"

He closed the distance between them much
quicker than she'd have expected for someone still
recovering from a brutal beating. And then he was
threading a hand in her hair, tilting her head back,
his mouth coming down on hers—lightly, sweetly
because of the cut on her lip. It stung, and yet it
was also heaven.

Sensation crashed through her, tightening her
nipples, stretching her skin, leaving a fiery imprint in its wake. The kiss was nothing, and yet it
was everything. They were sharing breath, sharing heat and scent and touch.

He slipped his other arm around her, pulled her
close enough that she felt the hard hot heat of him
through the woven cotton of her robe. His tongue
traced the line of her lips, the touch sensual and
overwhelming, and she opened her mouth to let
him inside because she suddenly couldn't imagine
doing anything else.

When their tongues met, she couldn't stifle
the moan that emanated from her throat. He was

o cautious, so gentle, and yet she wanted more, vanted him to unleash the fire. But he remained gentle with her, his tongue stroking against hers o deliciously, not overtly demanding and yet so compelling at the same time.

It was an intimate caress, this sensual slide of ongues together, and she shivered with the lusciousness of it.

She threaded her fingers into his hair, pulled is mouth tighter to hers. The contact stung, and ret she wanted it, needed it somehow. The kiss deepened, and her insides liquefied. Her body iched with need. It had been so long since she'd been with a man. Yet that wasn't what caused the iche.

It was him. Jack Wolfe. He was exasperating and exciting and dangerous and tender. She couldn't figure him out, but she knew there was omething potent between them, something that vould likely consume them both if they gave in o it.

And she couldn't afford that kind of annihilation, not now. She had to keep her head, had to keep her heart intact. She had to do the job she'd igreed to do and then she needed to find work. Maybe she'd even find something in London. Even if it were only temporary, at least she would get to have the adventure she'd always wanted.

Everything was going well at home, and with

the money she was about to send, there would be
nothing left to worry over. She could finally see
the world on her terms.

Jack's hand slipped to the curve of her buttock,
cupped her, and a shiver of desire shot straight to
her core. His mouth grew bolder, more insistent,
and she clung to him, enjoying the heady feel of
his body against hers.

She trailed a hand down his arm, over his chest.
But when his hands went to the belt at her waist,
she stilled. What was she doing? How could she
allow this? He was paying her to go to London
with him, to attend a wedding, and she was about
to let him make love to her? Did he think it was
his right? Or was he simply acting according to
the moment?

Because she didn't know, she somehow found
the strength to push him away. "No, Jack. I can't,"
she said, aware that she didn't sound very certain
of herself.

If he pushed the point, she was afraid she would
succumb to his charm. Because he was handsome
and glorious and she was strangely susceptible to
him.

He gripped her upper arms, squeezed only a
moment and then set her back a step. His chest
rose and fell almost as quickly as hers did.

"I guess we know now, don't we?"

She looked up, met his gaze, her heart flipping at the intensity of those glittering silver eyes. "Know what?"

He tucked her hair behind her ear, ghosted his fingers along her jaw, let them trail down her neck. He stopped at the thrumming pulse point in her throat, smiled. It was a weary smile, a disappointed smile.

"That we could be very good for each other."

Cara tucked her hands into her folded arms, shivered. "Only in bed, Jack. And that's not enough, I'm afraid."

His head tilted as he studied her. She felt self-conscious, silly. Like a girl, not a woman. A skittish virgin. She wasn't the kind of woman who slept around, but she'd had her share of lovers. He made her feel like she had no experience whatsoever.

"You're looking for happy ever after, Cara?"

Her ears burned with embarrassment. It was so contrary to everything she'd ever experienced, and yet it was the truth. She *needed* to believe in true love, even if she'd never seen it. That he'd seen to the heart of the matter should surprise her, and yet it didn't. "Isn't everyone?"

"What if it doesn't exist?"

She worried about that, too. Because hadn't she thought that Mama and Daddy were happy?

Hadn't she thought they had a wonderful, loving marriage? Until Daddy betrayed them all and left Mama brokenhearted and alone.

In spite of all that had happened to damage her faith in men and relationships, she stubbornly clung to the hope she needed. There had to be more to life than simply existing. There just *had* to be. "It's a chance I'll have to take, I suppose."

He looked at her as if he pitied her. "Seems lonely."

Cara turned away. It was too much, too close to home. "Thank you for the clothes, Jack," she said, fingering the green sweater set.

He let out an exasperated breath, but she didn't turn to look at him. "I'll leave you to dress, then. When you're ready, we'll go out."

And then he was gone, the door closing behind him, and she was alone. Cara sank onto the edge of the bed, trembling with adrenaline and thwarted desire.

She was in so much trouble here. She had to be careful, had to watch herself. Or she'd end up doing something she would most certainly regret later. Jack Wolfe was a player, a man who loved women and fast cars and dangerous pursuits. He wasn't the kind of man to be interested in her any longer than it took to win the chase. He would bed her and be done with her.

And she was afraid she couldn't bear it if he no longer looked at her the way he did now.

"Stupid, Cara," she whispered. Then she got up and began to dress.

Paris was indeed a feast for the senses. Cara sat at the table on the patio of the small café where Jack had taken her for dinner and gaped at the sophisticated Parisians as they passed by. The table was small, intimate, tucked into a corner of the patio that no one else occupied. The linens were crisp and white, and the food smelled delicious. Cara had worried for a moment that she would feel uncomfortable in this chic city but everyone had been so friendly.

She felt so different in the clothes Jack had bought her, as if she were sophisticated and cultured, and she'd delighted in their reception at the café. The maître d', who'd treated her with absolute courtesy, seemed very happy to see Jack, as if he were a regular customer.

Which, she realized, he must be since he had an apartment nearby. Did he often bring his dates here? The thought was unwelcome. Not because she wanted to be the only woman he'd ever brought to this café, but because it was *her* experience of Paris—and she didn't want to imagine anyone else sharing her memory.

"Is there anything you don't like to eat?" Jack asked once they had been seated.

"I don't think so."

"Do you trust me to order, then?"

"Yes."

He ordered in rapid French and the first course arrived shortly after. Cara couldn't wait to take a bite of the delicate foie gras. She spread it on a cracker and popped it into her mouth.

"Oh, God," she said, closing her eyes as she chewed. "That's amazing."

"I'm glad you think so."

When the waiter returned, she asked him to pass her compliments to the chef.

"I didn't realize you spoke French," Jack said once the waiter was gone again.

Cara smiled. "There's a lot you don't know about me, Jack. I'm from New Orleans, *mon ami*. We speak French, though it's a very different kind of French than they speak here, I have to admit. Which is why I don't trot it out very often."

"You are Cajun, then?"

"Half. My mama is a Broussard."

"And your father?"

Cara's grip tightened on her fork. "Just a plain old Taylor. The Taylors were from Mississippi originally."

"You are very far from home, then," he said.

Not far enough sometimes, it seemed.

Cara swallowed guiltily. "You say that as if people don't ever travel anywhere."

"Yes, but you aren't traveling, precisely. You came to work."

Cara ducked her head, studied the pâté as she spread it over another cracker. "I wanted to experience new places. It's perfectly normal." She thrust her chin at him. "You're British, and yet you live here."

"This is only one of my homes."

Cara felt her jaw drop just a little. She snapped it closed again. "Gambling must be very good to you."

He laughed. "It can be."

"Aren't you afraid you'll lose it all on one turn of the cards?" Because she really didn't understand how he could do it, how he could risk so much and not blink an eye. She worked hard for every dime she had, and no way could she gamble it all on a turn of the cards or a roll of the die. Mama depended on her too much.

Jack shrugged. "Not especially. It hasn't happened yet. But, Cara, cards aren't how I make money."

She blinked. "They aren't?" Because he'd shown every sign of being a professional high roller.

"No." He took a drink of his wine. "I own an investment firm."

An investment firm. That seemed far more stable than gambler, and yet the knowledge didn't abate the feeling she had that Jack loved to take risks. Investing was simply another way to play the odds.

"I'm relieved to hear it," she said. "Once we part ways, I won't be worried that you'll be trying to rescue some other croupier from Bobby Gold's evil clutches."

He laughed, and she couldn't help but laugh with him. She loved the sound of his laugh, the way his voice grew richer and more potent when he did so. It was as if he needed a moment to figure out *how* to laugh, a moment to let his voice slide into the joy of doing so. It made her wonder if he didn't laugh very often, and yet that seemed an odd thought because he'd laughed easily enough with her since they'd been together.

"You're an amusing woman, Cara Taylor."

"I try," she said, breaking a piece of bread and slathering it with butter. "So what about you, Jack? Where are your roots?"

His expression morphed, grew more cautious. Shadows drifted across his eyes. Cara shivered inwardly. With the blackened skin under one eye, it made him seem so dark and dangerous and hopeless.

What had happened to the light? The beautiful light was gone now, replaced by a mask of indifference. It made her sad to see him like this.

"I'm British."

"I know that." Her heart pounded in her ears as she tried to make him laugh again with her tone. It didn't work.

"My parents are dead," he said, his fingers toying with the stem of his wineglass. He looked so remote and untouchable, nothing like the man who'd been gently teasing her only moments ago. Nothing like the man who'd kissed her so passionately earlier.

"I'm sorry."

He shrugged. "Don't be. My mother died when I was three. I don't remember anything about her. And my father..."

He didn't say anything else for the longest time. And then he looked up, caught her gaze. Shrugged again. But his eyes...

His eyes burned so hot and dark that it made her reach for her wine. She took a gulp, let the acidic dryness scour her throat.

"My father died twenty years ago," he said. "But it wasn't soon enough for me."

CHAPTER SIX

JACK couldn't believe he'd told her he was glad his father was dead. He'd never said it to anyone other than Jacob. Never voiced the words that damned him.

Cara's eyes were wide as she watched him. Now was the time when she would protest his cruelty, tell him he couldn't really mean it. She would be shocked, disgusted. She would want to leave, want to pull out of their arrangement.

He would let her go.

Because it was best, because she brought things out in him that shocked him, as well. He couldn't quite control himself around her. Couldn't control his impulses or needs. And that was dangerous, because he was a man who was always in control. Rigid self-control was one of the hallmarks of his success. He had the ability to stay in the game far longer than another man, because he controlled the fear of failure.

Men who feared made decisions based on that

fear. Jack feared nothing. And because he feared nothing, he always won.

Cara reached across the table, grazed his hand. His skin sizzled where she touched, the current arcing between them with unbearable heat. He wanted so badly to bury himself in her sweet, lush body. To spend himself in a long, hazy, crazy night of hot lovemaking.

But he clamped down on the ferocious need, because her need was different. Because she would despise him now, after what he'd said. He hadn't said the words exactly, but she understood.

I hated him. I'm glad he's dead.

"I'm sorry, Jack."

"Sorry for what? That he's dead or that I'm glad?"

She withdrew her hand, sighed. "Sorry that you feel that way. Because you must have your reasons, and so I'm sorry for them, whatever they are."

The traffic zipped by on the street, hardly slowing. He was used to it, used to the idea that the world continued spinning without care while you felt as if it had left you behind somehow. He wanted it to stop, wanted to get back on board. But it never did. It never had.

"You aren't shocked?" he asked.

Her eyes were so liquid, so warm and sad all at once. She shook her head. "No."

Something flooded him, some feeling of relief and anger and pain all combined. Why? "You're an odd woman, Cara Taylor."

One corner of her mouth lifted in a soft smile. "You just told me I was an amusing woman. Which one is it?"

He couldn't help but shake his head at the wonder of her. "Both, I think." And then he reached for her hand, lifted it to his lips and pressed a kiss on the back before turning it over and kissing her palm.

He heard the intake of her breath, that slight catch that said she was as aroused as he was by the contact. "Jack..."

"I want you, Cara."

She bit her lip, her skin flushing a delicate pink. It was such a sweet, innocent reaction—and it fired his blood, made him harder than the marble tabletop.

"I'm not ready for this," she said. "So much has happened in the past twenty-four hours—"

"You need time." His body ached for hers, and yet he knew that he shouldn't push her. It wasn't fair to push her. Perhaps, if last night had been normal, they'd have fallen into bed together and it would all be over. He'd be on his way to England, and she'd be getting ready to go to the casino. "I understand."

"Do you really? Because I get the impression

you're very accustomed to getting what you want when you want it."

He kissed her warm skin again, then let her hand go. "Some things are worth waiting for."

She pushed a strand of her long, silky brunette hair over her shoulder. The sweater the boutique had sent up looked amazing on her. It brought out the green in her eyes, the cream of her skin. The woman at the boutique had asked what Cara's coloring was. He hadn't realized the results would be quite so spectacular when he'd described her eyes and hair.

"I like you, Jack. But I'm not sure sleeping with you is a good idea. This is a business arrangement, nothing more."

A thought occurred to him then. Something he'd not thought of before because she seemed so earthy, so sensual, even while she had that edge of innocence.

"Are you still a virgin?"

She bit her lip, looked away. "No, I'm not. But that doesn't mean I'm in the habit of falling into bed with strange men." When she swung her gaze to him again, she looked fierce, determined. "I don't need to be a virgin to want to exercise caution."

"And here I thought I was irresistible," he drawled, more to make her laugh than anything. He didn't know why he liked making her laugh, why he laughed when he was with her. He wasn't the laughing kind, not usually.

"Incorrigible, maybe," she said.

Yes, he was definitely that. Hopeless. Irredeemable. Most definitely irredeemable. "This isn't over, Cara."

"I didn't think it was. I'd be stupid to think so."

"Then you must realize the truth." Because there was no denying it, no possibility of denying it when the electricity snapped between them so strongly that the air was saturated with it.

"What truth is that, Jack?"

"That you want me, every bit as much as I want you. And we *will* end up in bed together, sooner or later."

Cara studied Jack as he stood on the deck of the boat they'd boarded to cruise the Seine. He looked comfortable, at ease, and yet she sensed the undercurrent flowing through him. He was a complex man. He was both very approachable and extremely distant. She had the feeling that if she spent years with him, she might never really know him.

And that saddened her most of all. Because she wanted to know him, wanted to understand how he could hate the man who'd fathered him. She didn't hate her own father, but she was bitterly, erribly angry with him. She knew how those feelings could take root deep inside and never leave you.

She didn't doubt Jack had reasons, good reasons, for the way he felt. But it worried her to imagine what they might be.

It was growing dark now, but the night lights of Paris were incredible against the blue-black sky. She tried to enjoy the sights, the Notre Dame Cathedral, the famous stone bridges, the people who walked beside the river, engrossed in conversation or, in some cases, kissing.

But it was difficult with Jack standing so close, with the remnants of their conversation so fresh in her mind. She wanted to go into his arms, wanted to stand in his embrace while the city slid by. She pulled her sweater tighter around her. April in Paris was colder than she'd realized.

Jack turned to look at her, as if he were somehow attuned to her distress. Without a word, he put his arm around her and pulled her close.

"Your ribs," she said.

"This side is fine. It's the other side that's bruised. Touch me there, I might scream like a little girl."

She couldn't help but laugh. "It's not funny."

"I'm not the one laughing, am I?"

"Jack."

He grinned and turned to look at the sights

again. She thought he must be somewhat bored, since he had a home here and had surely done this before. It was such a touristy thing to do.

It warmed her, the knowledge he would do such a thing for her. It was getting late—perhaps he'd prefer to be home, soaking his battered body in the tub again. But he was here, and she was having a marvelous time.

After they'd finished dinner, he'd taken her shopping. She'd been so embarrassed, so unsure, but he'd told her it was okay, told her to let the shopgirls help her. He'd offered to leave if it made her more comfortable, but she'd told him no. She'd felt as if she would be hopelessly lost if he weren't there. Her French was passable, but it was quite different from the French spoken here. The accents she'd grown up with, the lovely thick rolling of the tongue, the inclusion of Creole and other immigrant languages in the vocabulary, made communication a little more difficult when precision was required.

And she wanted to be precise when it came to her clothing.

"I don't want to spend more than two thousand," she'd told him, her pulse thrumming. It was a huge sum to spend on clothes, and yet she'd thought a smaller number wouldn't work in the kinds of boutiques they'd been in.

He'd given her that devilish grin. "Let me worry about that."

She shook her head adamantly. "No. Take it from what you're paying me already. I insist."

"Then we'll do it your way," he'd said without argument.

The boxes and bags had added up after she'd tried on several outfits. She'd grown suspicious then, insisted she didn't need so much for a wedding, but he'd overridden her protests.

"We'll do an accounting later, when I pay you," he said. And then he'd arranged for everything to be taken back to his place and brought her on board this boat.

She tilted her head up to look at his handsome profile. "This is nice, Jack. Thank you."

His warm body was comforting. She wanted to press even closer, but she dared not. For two reasons. One, she wasn't sure he was telling the complete truth about his ribs, and two, it was dangerous to want to be close to him. Dangerous for her peace of mind, for her willpower.

He'd said they would end up in bed together sooner or later. She knew he was probably right, and yet she was determined to fight it as long as possible. Because she knew it wouldn't be completely casual for her. He was a typical man, of course. He wanted into her panties. Once he'd gotten there, his desire for her would abate. She'd no longer be interesting, amusing or any of the other things he thought she was at the moment.

She'd just be another notch on his bedpost.

And the more time she spent with him, the less she could be satisfied with a casual encounter.

Really, Cara?

It was insane, and yet she knew it was the truth. Jack Wolfe was wrong for her—and yet she wanted him to be right. There was far more to him than she'd thought just yesterday—was it really only yesterday?—when he'd flirted with her at the casino.

But he was way out of her league. He was rich, amazingly so, and she was just a poor girl from New Orleans. She wasn't the kind of woman he'd truly be interested in. It bothered her, that feeling of not being good enough. Rationally, she knew she was a good person, a person worthy of love and tenderness.

But life had been so hard the past few years. Reality had crashed down when Katrina blew it to pieces over top of her. Until then, Mama and Daddy had sheltered her and Remy and Evie, provided for them, and made life seem so full of possibilities.

She'd been planning to go to college, to work her way through community college first and then apply to Tulane. Until Katrina had stolen her house and family away. Daddy had walked out, and nothing was ever the same again.

How could he have done it? How could he have lied for so long and left them once the truth was out? He'd chosen his other family over them, and she could never forgive him for it. She hadn't spoken a word to him in almost six years. Didn't expect she ever would again.

She stole another glance at Jack. Was he trustworthy? Or was he the sort of man who could turn his back on everything and everyone he'd known? She just didn't know if she could ever trust any man again. Daddy, James, Bobby—they'd all promised her things, and they'd all broken those promises. Jack would break his promises, too, if she were to allow him into her life any more deeply than he already was.

"What are you thinking?" he asked, turning his head to look down into her eyes.

She shrugged. "I was just thinking about how wonderful it is to be here, to see things I've only ever read about."

One dark eyebrow arched. "Is that all?"

"Have you ever been married?" she blurted, surprising herself as much as him. Now where had that come from?

"No." His voice grew chilly when he said it, as if in warning. *Careful where you tread, little girl.*

"Why not?" She wanted to know. She wasn't sure what knowing the answer would tell her about him, but maybe it would tell her something.

"Why the questions, Cara?"

"I'm trying to get to know you. You're rich, successful, and it seems as if you would have been married with a family by now."

His nostrils flared as he turned his head to look out over the dark water. "I guess I didn't want the responsibility."

Of all the answers he could have given, that was somehow the worst. He didn't want the responsibility. Because being a rich playboy was easier. He didn't need to care about anyone but himself. He could change women the way he changed clothes. He could drive fancy cars, stay out all night and get beaten up trying to rescue damsels in distress—even if the damsel preferred to rescue herself. He wasn't the kind of man who would ever be happy tied down. He was exactly as she'd thought: unreliable for more than the moment, however long the moment lasted.

"What about you, Cara? Have you ever been married?"

The question startled her, probably because she hadn't expected him to turn it back on her. But she could answer honestly. "No, not yet."

"Never been close?"

She shook her head. "There's been no one that important."

"That surprises me," he said. "What about the boyfriend you went to Vegas with? He must have been important if you were willing to leave home for him."

"Maybe I thought so at first," she said, staring out over the dark water. "But I realized he wasn't."

"When he ran off with the showgirl?"

"No, when I realized he was just an excuse."

"An excuse?"

How could she tell him how desperately she'd wanted to escape Louisiana without it sounding bad? Without it sounding like she'd abandoned her family because she felt hemmed in by responsibility?

Did it even matter? Why did she care what he thought? She hadn't abandoned them at all. She'd actually made things better by going somewhere that she could make more money. Because she had, her family was doing better than ever. They were no longer desperate to make ends meet.

"He was the excuse I needed to leave," she said coolly. "I needed the shove out the door, and he provided it."

"Ah," he said. "And yet you still believe in happy ever afters."

She refused to be embarrassed over it. "I think it's possible, yes. Don't you?"

"No, I don't."

Cara resisted the urge to snort. Of course he wouldn't believe in love that lasted forever. Jack lived in the moment. And yet she felt like challenging him on it.

"What about this wedding we're going to? Don't you believe they'll be happy together?"

"I hope so. Nathaniel deserves happiness."

Interestingly, she was incensed for Nathaniel, whoever he was. "Does Nathaniel know you don't give him very good odds of being happy with his new wife?"

Jack's expression was wry. "I doubt he cares. He's always done what he wanted. My opinion doesn't matter much."

"Sensible man," she said. "How long have you known him?"

"All my life. He's my brother."

Her heart skipped a beat. He was taking her to a family wedding? She'd thought it was just a wedding, not a family function. It had seemed so much easier when it had been simply *a wedding*.

"What's the matter?" he asked when she didn't say anything.

Cara swallowed. "I didn't realize I'd be meeting your family. That seems much more personal than a business arrangement."

"It's not. We're not a very close family."

Something in his tone made her heart ache. She wasn't close to her father, not anymore, but she couldn't imagine life without Mama and Remy and Evie. It was true she wanted adventure, true she wanted to explore and do her own thing, but to not have them to go home to? To not have that safe haven that would always be there, especially now that she'd done so much to secure it for them?

It was unthinkable.

"I see this surprises you," he said. "And yet, here you are, thousands of miles from home."

"I left for many reasons, but we're still very close."

His gaze roamed her face. "Yes, I believe that. There's a light in your eyes whenever you mention them. And you've clearly worked very hard to provide for them."

"I love them," she said. And then, because she couldn't stop herself, she asked, "Aren't you ever lonely, Jack?"

His expression was tired, bleak. She saw the wounded warrior now, the man behind the mask—or were there more masks, more layers of obfuscation? It wouldn't surprise her if there were.

"I've been alone too long to be lonely," he said.

"That's ridiculous. How can you say that?"

He traced the line of her jaw with two fingers. "You're very naive, Cara. We don't all need the company of others to make our lives complete."

She bristled. "I choose to think of myself as optimistic. There's nothing wrong with hoping for the best. Nothing wrong with wanting to share my life with someone."

The boat thudded against the rubber bumpers of the dock, signaling that the ride was over. Jack stepped back, took her hand in his as if she were a child.

"Wait," she said when he tried to lead her toward the gangway. He gave her that look she was getting to know so well, the one that said he was annoyed but tolerating her. Well, nothing said she had to stand for it. She wasn't letting him barrel through her life, giving orders and making plans—which was what he'd been doing since he'd walked in and sat down at her table last night.

"I'm not naive, Jack. Wanting more out of life and relationships is not naive. I'm a big girl, I know what I want."

He inclined his head. "No, maybe it's not naive to know what you want out of life. If only more people did. But, Cara, wanting more out of *me* is very naive."

"I didn't say anything about you, did I?" she threw at him. "Honestly, your arrogance is unbelievable sometimes."

She didn't wait for him to reply. She strode up the gangway, tears pricking at the backs of her eyes as a shiver of premonition skimmed up her spine. Because, damn her, she did want more from him. She wanted there to be something else besides this incredible heat and pull of attraction between them. She wanted there to be the possibility of a relationship at the very least. Even if it didn't work out, she wanted to know he would take her seriously for more than the time it took to get her into bed.

Honest to God, she should just leave. She should tell him the deal was off. But where would she go? She couldn't go back to Nice, and she couldn't leave Europe without her passport.

Cara shook her head angrily. For now, she would stay. She had no choice but to stay.

And she would remember that Jack Wolfe was off-limits, no matter how her silly heart wanted the possibility of more. He was hiding behind walls that were stacked to the sky and thicker than the duckweed that choked the bayous back home. The rare glimpses she'd gotten behind those walls were carefully controlled constructs that he trotted out for the sake of appearances.

No, the real Jack was buried too deep to ever break free. She didn't really know him—and she probably never would.

CHAPTER SEVEN

THEY spent another full day in Paris before setting out for London on a private plane only a few hours before the wedding. Cara had never flown in such luxury before. The plane was furnished in blue and cream, its plush chairs overstuffed and comfortable. There was plenty of legroom, a table in front of her that didn't require anyone to fold down a tray and a sleek chrome bar where a uniformed attendant was stacking drinks in a refrigerator.

She'd hoped to take the train so she could experience the Chunnel, but Jack had informed her that her lack of a passport would be a problem. They were flying because, presumably, Jack knew people. At least she hoped he did, because she'd hate to be sent back to France when he'd gone to so much trouble.

"How does one go about renting a private plane?" she asked. The engines spooled up as they began to taxi down the runway.

"I own it," he said.

Cara could only stare at him. He owned a plane? *A plane?* She glanced around the interior. It seemed even more lush and rich than it had only moments ago. *My God.*

Jack picked up a copy of a British newspaper and flipped it open. Cara turned to look out the window while the plane gathered speed, shooting down the runway before lifting into the air in a stomach-dropping ascent. She glanced at Jack, but he didn't seem in the least perturbed. She hadn't flown often, and the experience was still both exhilarating and frightening every time.

As the plane climbed, she watched the countryside below. It was so beautiful, and vastly different than her home in Louisiana. Here, there were vineyards, cows, verdant fields and stone villages in abundance. At home, there would be swamps, a lot of flat wetlands, sand and pine trees.

A flight attendant came over and asked if she would like a drink. When the woman returned with a glass of iced water, Cara thanked her, hoping she didn't look as unsophisticated as she felt.

Real glass on an airplane instead of plastic. A man who owned an airplane. Wealth and luxury like she'd never imagined she would ever personally experience. She'd seen plenty of luxury in the casinos, but she'd never expected to be on the other end of the luxury. Enjoying it as if she were entitled to it.

She felt like a fraud.

"Want the paper?" Jack asked.

Cara jerked her attention toward him. He'd finished the paper. The sections lay neatly folded on the table between them. She shook her head. "No, thanks." A moment later, she asked, "Do you think you might tell me a little bit about who will be at this wedding?"

"Scared, Cara?" The skin under his eye was black and blue, but he was still so handsome in his dark Italian suit. She ran a hand over the turquoise jersey dress she'd chosen for the wedding, marveling at the weight and texture of the fabric. At least she wouldn't look as if she didn't belong.

When she'd emerged in the dress this morning, Jack's eyes had gleamed hotly as his gaze slid over her body. She loved the way he looked at her, and yet it frightened her, too. Because she was coming to expect that little electric jolt, to need it, and she knew it wouldn't last. What happened when they were through with this wedding?

She would have to go, would have to break away from this pull between them, if she hoped to survive with her heart intact.

"A little bit," she admitted. "But I think I'll feel more awkward than anything."

Jack's expression said he didn't understand why

she should. "There's not much to tell. Nathaniel is marrying a woman he met while doing his last play, I believe."

"Is he an actor? Or maybe a playwright?"

Jack's brows drew together as he studied her. "You've never heard of Nathaniel Wolfe? You are quite sheltered, aren't you?"

Cara suddenly couldn't breathe. Nathaniel Wolfe? Jack's brother was the award-winning actor? She was going to *his* wedding?

The panic she'd been holding in unwound in her belly. Oh, God, they'd see right through her! There'd be paparazzi, gossip columnists, movie people—and they'd all know she didn't belong. She couldn't possibly go to a *celebrity* wedding.

Cara gave herself a firm mental shake before she did something asinine like hyperventilate. Why on earth would any of those people care about her? They wouldn't. It was she who cared, she who was afraid. No one would even notice her.

Jack watched her, one eyebrow arched. As if he were waiting for her to implode. She refused to give him the satisfaction. She could handle this, she really could.

"I know who he is. I just didn't realize he was your brother," she said coolly. And now that she knew, she could see the family resemblance. Jack was older, she thought, but just as devastatingly handsome. More so, in her opinion. She didn't follow celebrity news at all, but she knew there'd been some sort of scandal about Nathaniel Wolfe, something to do with his father's death at the hands of a brother and sordid details about his mother trying to drown him when he was a baby.

Cara shivered. My God, Jack had grown up in that family?

"Nathaniel is my half brother," Jack said. "We had different mothers. Sebastian, another half brother, will likely be there, as well. Alex won't be there, but his twin—Annabelle—will. The three of us have the same mother."

"So you have four siblings." She couldn't remember how many Wolfes there were from the news reports. They'd never featured Jack, or surely she would have remembered that.

She realized he was in no hurry to respond. He flicked a spot on his trousers, studying it as if he'd found a blemish. When he looked up again, his eyes were startlingly blank.

"There are eight of us. Rafael is also my half brother, as are the two oldest, Jacob and Lucas."

"Wow, eight of you, then." Jacob. That was the brother who'd accidentally killed their father. As soon as he'd said the name, she'd remembered reading it. Her heart squeezed for the man sitting across from her. He was so stoic, so controlled.

She wanted to hug him, but knew he wouldn't welcome the contact.

He gave a curt nod. It was clear he didn't want to talk about it. Clear he'd already said more than he wanted to say. And she had no wish to keep probing his wounds. *Oh, Jack…*

"Is there anything else I should know?"

"That about sums it up," he said dispassionately, as if they were talking about the weather or game scores. "Except for Annabelle. Her face is scarred, though she hides it quite well. You probably won't even notice, but in case you do…"

Cara drew herself up. "I would never be so crass as to ask her what happened!"

He sighed. "Of course not. Forgive me."

The bubble of her indignation popped. He was under a lot of stress, and she should have let it go without comment. "No, I should apologize. I'm sorry for snapping. For all you know about me, I might just be that rude. But I'm not, you can rest assured."

He nodded once, and then they lapsed into silence again. The closer they got to their destination, the more withdrawn Jack became. Cara could feel the tension in the air like a huge coil spring being compressed tighter and tighter and tighter. It was as if the miles piled up on his shoulders, their weight pressing him deeper and deeper into the ground.

She wished she could remember more of the details about his family, but she'd hardly paid attention to the fuss. It was all very recent, she remembered, but she'd been so busy working and then coming to Nice to open the new casino. She barely had time to check her email, much less read celebrity gossip rags.

By the time they arrived in London—after their plane was delayed in the air because of a problem on the ground—Cara was worried that Jack really would come unsprung. She wouldn't have called him a carefree person by any stretch, but his demeanor now, compared with yesterday, was night and day. This Jack was dark, closed in, and she ached for him. Wanted so desperately to reach out to him.

And yet there was nothing she could do. Whatever demons awaited him, she could only go along for the ride. She would not abandon him now, not when he might need a friend.

After they emerged from the private airport they'd flown into, a limo was waiting to take them to the Grand Wolfe Hotel. Cara was no longer surprised at anything she learned about Jack and his family. Finding out he had a brother rich enough to own a hotel in central London was par for the course these days. Just like finding out that Jack was rich enough to own a plane.

Cara shook her head. She'd been so wrong about

im it was laughable. She'd always prided her-
elf on reading people, especially as she worked
ne casinos, but Jack Wolfe was not as he first
ppeared. He had the sharp eye and fearless de-
neanor of a professional gambler, and yet he was
o much more than a card shark.

After the delayed flight, they got caught in
eavy traffic on the ride to the hotel. Jack didn't
eem to notice. He stared out the window, his ex-
•ression distant. More than once, she almost sug-
ested they go back to the airport and return to
'aris. He'd been happy there; they'd been happy
ogether.

Now, he was so remote. A complete stranger to
er. It felt…odd.

Tentatively, she reached for his hand where
t rested on his thigh. Just to show him she un-
lerstood, that she was here. Her skin sizzled, as
lways, when her body made contact with his. He
urned his hand over, opening it, and then their
›alms were touching, fingers entwining. It wasn't
nuch, just a simple contact between two people
vho barely knew each other.

And yet it felt like everything, like their souls
intwined with their fingers. Cara turned her head
iway, the cars and sidewalks of London blurring
is she blinked back tears. She would not cry over
omething as simple as a touch. She would not
illow it to mean more than it did.

It was touch. Warmth, companionship, light Cara squeezed his hand gently. She didn't expect acknowledgment, didn't expect anything from him. But when he squeezed back, she knew she'd gotten through his shield, if only a tiny bit. It was a start.

Jack glanced at his watch as they arrived at the Grande Wolfe. He'd feared they would be late the instant they'd gotten delayed in the air. He'd planned his arrival to leave no time for socializing with his family. He'd made allowances for traffic, of course, but he'd not counted on the plane being late.

But he was here now and he had to get this over with. Had to go next door to the church for the ceremony, had to smile, had to be happy for Nathaniel—which he genuinely was—and had to hope Jacob avoided him. The last thing he needed was a confrontation with his brother.

Everyone else seemed glad—or at least resigned—that Jacob was back, glad that he'd returned to restore the broken-down manor where they'd grown up. But Jack couldn't care less about Wolfe Manor. Let it be torn down, let the past stay buried where it belonged.

Jacob hadn't cared about the place when he'd left them so many years ago, so why now? It was a ruse, quite simply, because Jacob didn't have staying power. Let the rest of them fall for Jacob's act, but Jack was not about to do so. If someone burned him once, they never got the chance to do so again.

Cara emerged from the limo and smiled up at him, and his world felt as if it were shifting somehow. It was the effect of what awaited him, he knew, and yet he was glad she was here with him.

A bellhop came to collect their luggage, and Jack took one last fortifying breath before grasping Cara's hand and walking next door to the church. The ceremony had probably already started, but they could sneak into the back and watch from there. Then they would escape with the first exodus and head for the hotel.

But the church was empty, except for a few ladies cleaning up. Jack blinked at the scene before him. A profusion of white roses decorated the pews and altar, their scent almost cloying. He pivoted and led Cara back outside.

She didn't speak as they headed into the depths of the hotel. He found the ballroom where the reception was being held easily enough, having stayed at Sebastian's hotel from time to time over the years, but the crowd was a bit lighter than he would have expected.

The room had been draped in white organza, and once more the scent of roses filled the air. A few people danced to the elegant sounds of the band, but the tables were only about half-full.

Jack spotted Annabelle almost immediately. She had her camera out, taking photos. She looked as coolly elegant as she always did. She glanced over, made eye contact with him. And then she was making her way toward them, her camera held like a shield in front of her body.

"You're late, Jack," she said as she walked up. Her gaze flicked over his face, but he knew she wouldn't comment on the bruise beneath his eye.

He gave her a brief hug. Annabelle didn't like to be touched, really, but he always felt so damn sorry for her that he wanted her to know he cared. She returned the hug as well as she was able before stepping back into her own space.

"There was a problem at the airport," he said. "Where are Nathanial and Katie?"

"They've left for their honeymoon already. You missed everything." Her voice was remarkably devoid of censure, but that was Annabelle. Cool and collected to the last.

Jack wasn't sure if he was relieved or disappointed. He'd known the timing was tight, but he hadn't thought they would miss *everything* once they were delayed. He'd thought to see at least a bit of the ceremony. Then a quick stop at the reception, and he'd be gone again before too much time had passed. He'd intended to congratulate the happy couple, to speak to Annabelle and Sebastian at least, and then to retire to his suite for the night. He hadn't wanted to insult Sebastian by refusing to stay in the hotel overnight, but as soon as he was able, he was taking Cara to his London home and leaving the Grand Wolfe behind.

He introduced Cara to Annabelle. They exchanged pleasantries, and then Annabelle said she needed to go and pack up her equipment.

"Did everyone come?" he asked her.

If she knew what he meant, she didn't let on. "Everyone but Alex. Oh, and Rafael came alone."

Jack shrugged. "Leila is probably working."

"Perhaps. But he didn't seem very happy."

They talked for a few moments more, and then Annabelle was gone.

Cara was biting her lip again. He knew she must be disappointed that they'd missed the wedding as she worried that plump lower lip between her teeth. He wanted her to stop, and he wanted to bite it for her. A shot of pure lust rocketed through his body at the thought of doing just that. Maybe it was a good thing they had a hotel room after all.

"I'm sorry you missed meeting Nathaniel," he said. Because he was certain, though she'd not said anything, that she'd been looking forward to meeting his famous brother. Who wouldn't want to meet a movie star?

"I'm not," she said softly, her eyes more green than gold as she gazed up at him. "But I am sorry you didn't see your brother get married."

Jack shrugged it off. He'd wanted to be here for Nathaniel, but he had no one to blame but himself. If he'd flown in earlier—or yesterday, like everyone else—there'd have been no problem. "I'll see him again soon enough. He's far more interested in his new wife than in his family, anyway. As it should be."

"I'm glad I got to meet your sister. She's very pretty. And very serious."

"She wasn't always so serious," he said before he could stop himself.

If Cara wondered at that statement, she didn't allow her curiosity to show.

"So now what?" she asked, her pretty mouth curving in a soft smile. God, he loved her smiles. And he loved that she understood when he didn't want to talk about something. How could he tell her about the ugliness that had taken Annabelle's sweet innocence away forever?

Jack's eyes skimmed over her. The jeweled turquoise of her dress was magnificent. The fabric hugged her curves, displayed her assets to perfection. She had long legs, beautiful and toned, and he couldn't help but imagine them wrapped around him. He *wanted* them wrapped around him in the worst way.

Now that the tension of being here for the wedding was leaching away, a different kind of tension was taking its place. He wanted this woman, wanted to sweep her up and take her to the room where he would slowly reveal every inch of her delightful body. And then he would make love to her for hours, exploring her, learning her taste and texture, finding out what made her sigh with delight and scream with pleasure.

His body was stone. Pure, hard marble.

And yet he knew he couldn't rush this, knew he wasn't quite in the right state of mind just yet.

"How about a drink in the bar?" he said. "We can't have got all dressed up for nothing."

"That sounds good."

They made their way back toward the sleek bar on the other side of the lobby. Heads turned as they passed, and he knew it was because of the gorgeous brunette at his side. They'd just found a table and sat down when Jack saw Jacob watching him from across the bar.

White-hot fury exploded inside him with a force he was unprepared for. The first time he'd seen Jacob's face in how many years? Nearly twenty goddamn years. Jacob was older—they all were—but his face was still so familiar. It was a shock on so many levels to see Jacob, and yet anger was by far the dominant emotion churning through Jack.

"Jack, what's wrong?" Worry laced Cara's voice, but he couldn't tear his gaze away from Jacob to answer her.

Jacob looked so cool, so unflappable. So goddamn smug.

Hatred boiled inside his gut, his brain, hatred that threatened to rip him apart at the seams it was so strong. And more. He didn't want to acknowledge the more, but he knew what it was. Disappointment, betrayal, rage, fear. Love.

It was the love that was worst of all. Knowing the love was dead and gone and there was nothing left but emptiness where a brotherly bond should have been.

He stood abruptly. "I changed my mind. Let's get a drink in our room," he said, holding his hand out to Cara.

Her brows drew together as she studied him. Then she sighed and unfolded those impossibly long legs.

Jack looked over to the bar again, but Jacob was gone. Cara was on her feet when the crowd parted and he caught sight of Jacob. His older brother was coming straight for him, his strides purposeful.

Jack's first instinct was to meet Jacob with a fist to the face. But he wouldn't do it. He was better than that, and he wouldn't allow Jacob to see how affected he truly was.

"Jack—"

"Get the hell away from me, Jacob," he burst out. "I don't want to talk to you. The time for talking was when you decided it would be easier to abandon us than stick with us and do your duty. I have *nothing* to say to you."

Jacob looked almost serene as he endured Jack's tirade—which only made Jack angrier. Then Jacob held up his hands, as if to put a stop to the torrent of words.

"I understand this is a shock," Jacob said, "but I can see that now isn't the time. I'll talk to you when you've calmed down."

Jack took a step toward his brother, violence radiating through every cell, every nerve ending. "When *I've* calmed down? I'm not the one who ran away when I couldn't take the pressure! You can have nothing to say to me, Jacob. Nothing I want to hear."

Jacob's lips compressed, but then he nodded and turned away. Jack watched his brother's retreating back. Anger whipped through him, followed by frustration and even that old, childish sense of abandonment. Jacob had been the closest thing he'd had to a father figure.

"Jack? Are you ready?"

He felt Cara's hand on his arm, the comforting

weight of it, the solidity of her body beside him. People in the bar had turned to look at them, but they turned away now that the drama was finished.

"Jack?"

She was looking up at him with a mixture of concern and tenderness. He put his hand over hers where it rested on his sleeve. Any other time, he'd want to be alone. This time, strangely, he did not.

"Yeah, let's go."

They were sharing a suite, Cara realized, but she didn't protest. The suite was luxurious, with a giant king-size bed and a couch in the living area for her to sleep on. She could have insisted on her own room now that he no longer needed her help for anything, but she couldn't leave him, not like this. She wasn't exactly certain what had happened in the bar, but the effect on Jack had been extraordinary.

He'd lost his temper, something she'd not seen him do even when threatened by Bobby and his men. He'd punched one of Bobby's guys, yes, but he'd been in control the whole time. The Jack she knew never lost control. But he had just now—spectacularly. She'd thought he was going to launch himself at Jacob. She didn't know anything about what had happened between them, but clearly it weighed heavily on Jack's mind. Had done so for years.

Jack stood by the window, hands thrust into his pockets. He hadn't spoken a word since they'd left the bar.

"Do you want me to order drinks from room service?" she asked. It wasn't that she wanted a drink, but she needed to say something, needed to fill the oppressive silence and see if she could get him talking again.

Anything to get him talking.

He glanced over at her. "Sure."

"What do you want?" She flipped through the menu, pretending a casualness she didn't feel. If she seemed normal, maybe he'd relax. Maybe he'd even open up to her. It wasn't likely, she acknowledged, but it was worth a try.

"Order a bottle of champagne," he said. "Or whatever you prefer."

"Champagne is fine." Cara picked up the phone and dialed room service. She'd never ordered room service in her life, had certainly never stayed in a hotel of this magnificence. The walls were papered in pale blue silk. The chandelier in the center of the suite was an ornate Venetian glass concoction shaped to look like flowers budding from a vase. The glass was multihued, beautiful beyond description.

There was a watered-silk chesterfield sofa

flanked by two modern leather chairs sitting on the biggest oriental carpet she'd ever seen. Sleek glass-topped tables rounded out the living area. Huge silk panels hung on the windows, held back by ornate tassels.

It was without doubt the most luxurious hotel room she'd ever been inside. While she waited for the champagne to arrive, Cara drifted over to the antique desk. She recognized the style as French because she'd seen furniture like this back in New Orleans. It was polished walnut, inlaid with flowers and scrolls. Cara sank into the upholstered chair and opened the drawers one by one, just for something to do.

A deck of cards lay in the center drawer. She took them out and flipped open the box. The backs had London landmarks on them. Quickly, she shuffled, loving the feel of the cards in her hands. She was *good* at what she did, dammit. It wasn't fair that she'd had to leave the way she had, that she might never work in a casino again. Because Bobby had reach, that was a certainty. Not only would he never hire her again, he might also have her blacklisted in every casino she ever tried to work in.

A knock sounded on the door and she got up to answer. A man wheeled in a trolley with a champagne bucket and two glasses. Deftly, he opened the champagne and poured some in each glass.

Jack came over and handed the man some cash, and then he was gone.

Cara sipped her champagne and watched Jack. He took his glass over to the window and downed it.

"I found a deck of cards," she said as she took the bottle over and poured him another drink. "Why don't we play a hand or two of poker?"

His gaze swung toward her.

"I know you're used to winning," she said, "but you've never played me. I'll try not to embarrass you, though."

Jack couldn't resist a challenge. And she was going to challenge him if that's what it took. She didn't know if she could really beat him, but he didn't need to know she wasn't confident. She *was* good at cards, no doubt about it. And she was damn good at bluffing.

"What are the stakes?" he asked, and her heart soared. She'd intrigued him enough to shake him from his brooding.

"If I win, you take me to some awful touristy thing that I'd love, but you hate."

"For instance?"

"I don't know." She cast about wildly, thinking of the sort of nutty things they'd had in Las Vegas, before making up something suitable for London. "A Jack the Ripper ghost walk. Or a Henry VIII turkey-leg banquet."

He almost grinned, she was certain. "And if I win?"

Cara shrugged. "We go somewhere you want instead."

"Doesn't sound like much incentive," he said, taking a sip of the champagne.

His eyes narrowed, his gaze slipping over her body. Her skin warmed, her nipples tightening beneath the fabric of her dress. Any second and he would know the effect he was having on her.

"I have a better idea," he said as his eyes met hers again.

"What's that?"

"We play for the clothes on our backs. Or we don't play at all."

CHAPTER EIGHT

CARA'S heart thundered in her ears. Strip poker. Could she do it? Because she knew what would happen if she lost.

Her body felt tight, achy, the tender area between her thighs melting, softening. Her body craved his so strongly it scared her. If they ended up in bed together, she didn't know what would happen after, but she feared he would be finished with her. This lovely feeling she had when she was with him would die.

And she wasn't ready for that to happen just yet.

Cara took a deep breath. But she wouldn't lose. She had just as good a chance of winning as he did. Maybe better, because she'd played from the other side of the table for so long that she had an instinctive feel for how things would shake out.

"Fine," she said. "We play for clothes."

Jack smiled for the first time in hours. It was a devilish smile, a supremely confident smile.

Warmth curled inside her belly, flooded her limbs.

"There's only one problem," she continued.

"What's that?"

"You're wearing more clothes than I am. Either you spot me a couple of hands, or you count that jacket, shirt and tie as one item."

He shrugged out of the jacket and tossed it on a nearby chair. "The shirt and tie count as one item."

She tipped her chin to his waistline. "And the belt?"

"Goes with the pants."

Cara picked up the deck of cards. If it got his mind off of what had just happened, if it gave her back the man she'd come to know, she'd risk it. "All right, then. I guess we're on. If you pull one of those chairs over here, we can play at the desk."

"The bed, Cara. It's bigger."

Her ears felt hot. Not from embarrassment, but from sensual overload. She *wanted* to play strip poker on a bed with this man. And she wanted to win, because she wanted to see that magnificent body again.

"Fine." She picked up her champagne. "Let's go."

"After you."

She led the way into the bedroom, set the

champagne on the bedside table and kicked off her heels before climbing onto the bed. When she turned around, Jack was watching her, his eyes smoky with desire.

"We could just skip the cards," he said, his deep voice vibrating over her nerve endings. "Save a whole lot of time and trouble."

"On the bed, Jack. Get ready to lose your shirt."

He slipped out of his shoes and socks, then got onto the bed opposite her. The center of the king-size bed was a good playing surface, if a little unorthodox. Cara shuffled the cards and Jack cut. Then she dealt with quick, practiced movements.

"I love watching your hands stroke those cards," Jack said.

"No trying to distract the dealer," she answered coolly. Then she picked up her hand.

She glanced at Jack—except that he was looking at her, as well. Both trying to gauge the other's reaction for a clue to the hand they held.

"You're a good bluffer," Jack said.

Cara arched an eyebrow. "Who says I'm bluffing?"

"I can always read people, but you're good at hiding your emotions at the table. I noticed that in Nice."

"Practice," she said, though her heart was

tripping along with adrenaline. No doubt his proximity had an effect, as well.

Jack tossed two cards down and smiled. Cara looked at her hand again. She had two fives, which was good, but she hoped for better.

Tossing three away, she dealt the next round. This time she picked up an ace, a two and another five. It wasn't stellar, but it was a good hand.

"Call," Jack said.

Cara laid down the cards. Jack only smiled. She'd seen that smile before, when Bobby's man had thought he'd won the pot. Then Jack laid down his hand. She scanned it desperately, relief flooding her when she realized he'd lost.

"Three of a kind beats two," she said.

"As I see it, there can be no losers here."

"Your shirt, please."

Jack's smile sent a shot of pure lust straight to her center as he began to loosen his tie. A second later he tugged it free and tossed it at her. Slowly, he unbuttoned the crisp white shirt he was wearing.

"You have a T-shirt on under that!" she exclaimed as the shirt fell open to reveal another layer beneath.

"You should have thought of it before. Too late now." He peeled the shirt off and dropped it on the floor.

Dammit, why did men wear so many more garments when they were dressed up than women did? It hardly seemed fair. She hadn't even worn stockings, which she was now regretting. But in the South, the weather was too oppressive to wear stockings; she'd gotten used to going without them whenever she wore a dress. Besides, her legs were good enough that she didn't need them.

Fortunately, Jack lost the next round, as well, his straight falling victim to her flush. He didn't seem quite as perturbed as she would have expected for losing two hands in a row and she began to wonder if he was doing it on purpose, toying with her to make her overconfident. She wouldn't put it past him, but she refused to be distracted by the ploy.

When he pulled the T-shirt over his head, Cara stifled a gasp. The skin on his left side was black and blue where Bobby's thugs had hit him.

"It looks worse than it is," he reassured her. "I have strong core muscles, which protected my ribs pretty well. Apparently, there is a benefit to working out."

Cara swallowed. The bruising did look brutal, and yet the smooth ridges of muscle were every bit as impressive as she recalled. He wasn't beefed up like a hard-core gym rat; rather, he was leanly muscled, sexy as hell. She wanted to run her tongue along those ridges.

Cara stifled her impulses and concentrated on

the cards. She had to be careful, or Jack would take her down so quick she wouldn't know what had hit her until too late.

But the next hand played out rapidly. The first clue she had that she'd lost was Jack's smug smile. Her gaze dropped to the cards. Two pair beat one pair. Damn.

"The dress, Cara," Jack said.

She thought about insisting on removing her panties instead—because at least she would have the coverage of the dress to protect her. But what if she lost another round? She couldn't get her bra off without removing the dress, so that would mean the dress would be next and she'd be sitting here in nothing but a bra.

Heat spread through her, permeating her bones, her blood, every cell of her body. But was it the heat of embarrassment or sexual heat?

She didn't know, but she shoved herself onto her knees and grasped the hem of her dress. Nothing left but to brazen it out. Because she wouldn't renege on a bet. Slowly, she peeled the dress upward, revealing her thighs, her belly, her breasts, before pulling it over her head and dropping it onto the bed.

Jack's eyes had darkened to pewter as he watched her. She knew what he was seeing. The white silk of her panties was thin, and the lacy demicups of her bra barely held her breasts in whenever she leaned forward. Her nipples had tightened some time ago. She had no doubt Jack could see the hard little bumps through the silk.

"Satisfied?" she asked.

"Hardly."

"I believe it's my turn to deal again," she said.

She gathered the cards, leaning forward just enough to make him think her breasts were about to pop free. It was a cheap shot to distract him, but she didn't care. Jack wasn't going to give her any quarter; she needed to be as ruthless as he was.

"I don't believe I've ever seen anything as sexy as a woman dealing cards in her underwear before," he said, his voice deep and husky with desire.

She looked up, her heart skipping a beat at the intensity of his stare. "I'm surprised," she replied. "I would have imagined you'd played this game quite often."

"I have," he said. "It doesn't usually last this long."

Cara blinked. "We've only played three hands."

He lifted one eyebrow, his expression smug, superior. Her insides quivered. "The women I've played in the past usually prefer to lose rather quickly. The good part is what comes after."

Cara tried not to imagine his naked body

stretched out beside another woman. On top o another woman. *Playboy. Player. Man-whore.*

She had to think of him that way, or she woul find herself in way over her head before this wa over with.

"That's nice," she said crisply. "Now pay at tention to the game and stop trying to distract m with sex." She shuffled the cards and handed him the deck to cut. "I'm not going to be so easy t beat."

Jack actually tsked as he cut the cards. "Haven' you figured it out yet, Cara?"

"Figured out what?" She took them back an swiftly dealt the next hand.

"That I never lose."

"Neither do I."

The next several hands passed with nothing happening, each one ending in a stalemate as on or the other of them folded. Jack got up from th bed. She watched his retreating back as he walke out into the living area, the way the muscles rip pled and bunched as he moved.

When he returned with the champagne bottle she forced herself not to stare.

"Sure is hot," he said. "More champagne?"

Cara nodded. She was dying of thirst, bu whether it was for liquid or because of him sh wasn't quite sure. He handed her the glass and sh took a small sip and set it on the nightstand. Sh planned to drink it very slowly so as not to let it interfere with her head.

Because Jack already interfered with her head just by being so close.

It was important to keep playing, and just as important to keep the rest of her clothes on. Jack had lightened up considerably since they'd started. She didn't fool herself he'd forgotten anything about what had happened in the bar with his brother. He'd merely shoved it to the back of his mind while he worked to beat the clothes off her body.

But he seemed happier, seemed like the Jack she'd come to know, and she liked that he wasn't brooding any longer. Whatever had happened with Jacob, it clearly still bothered him a very great deal. She wanted to know, and yet she knew she couldn't ask him. Not yet. Maybe not ever. What right was it of hers?

It wasn't. Why did that thought sadden her?

Jack sat down and picked up the cards. It was his turn to deal the next hand, which he did with efficient movements. Cara's pulse kicked higher at the three aces she held. Jack tossed down three cards.

Sweat beaded her upper lip as she picked up the two cards he dealt her. Relief surged through her: two sevens.

"What do you say, Cara?" Jack asked. "Your

bra against my trousers—or do you want to fold and preserve your dignity?"

Cara thrust her chin out. "Show me your hand, Jack."

"If that's what you want, sweetheart."

When his cards hit the bed, she let out a shaky breath.

"Oh, Jack," she said, laying her cards down oh so slowly, "I'm looking forward to seeing your legs again. Get to stripping, darling." She couldn't stop the smug grin that popped into place.

Jack lifted an eyebrow, gave her a quelling look. "So the kitten has claws, I see. Nicely done."

Then he stood and slipped open his belt. The sweat on her upper lip didn't abate. Though she was sitting on a bed in her underwear, her body was burning up. Especially when he unzipped his pants and shoved them down his hips.

He was wearing a pair of white briefs, and her gaze slid to the bulge in them. The very large bulge.

"I'm very ready for you, sweetheart," he said. "We can stop this game any time and get to the good part."

She wanted to. Oh, God, how she wanted to. But it was a bad idea. Bad because she wanted it so much. Bad because she'd never wanted a man this much, and had no idea what would happen if she let herself go with him. Would she fall in love? Would he break her heart?

Or would they have fantastic sex and go their separate ways as if it meant nothing at all?

Was she capable of meaningless sex?

She didn't think so. She'd never had a one-night stand, and she'd never slept with a guy she'd just met. She'd known Jack for three days—how could she possibly go to bed with him?

You're playing strip poker with the man, for God's sake! How could you not be prepared for the possibility of sex with him?

"I think you just don't like losing," she said.

He looked sinful, hot and dark and devilish. "I don't intend to lose, Cara."

"I'm not the one with only one stitch of clothing left," she retorted.

"Game's not over yet," he said. "Deal."

Cara picked up the cards and shuffled them. After he'd cut the deck, she dealt. The promise of the hand leached away with her next deal, so she folded. Three more hands passed with her folding each time.

"Are you trying to stave off the inevitable?" Jack asked.

"I haven't had a good hand," she said. "There isn't a time limit on this game, you know."

But another fifteen minutes passed before she got a hand she felt she could use. Only one card separated her from a flush. It was a risk, but when the next card came up diamonds, she breathed a sigh of relief. Inwardly, of course. She didn't want him to know she was confident in her hand.

This time, when the call came, she laid her cards down with a flourish. "Beat *that*."

His smile was not what she'd hoped to see. "I can do that," he said, spreading his cards out for her to see. A full house. Cara cursed inwardly. How had she let that happen? How had she not clued in to his body language on this one?

Because he was damn good, that's why. So was she. Usually.

"The bra," he said, eyes gleaming. "Off with it."

Heart tattooing the inside of her chest, she straightened her spine and reached behind her back to snap the bra open. Her nerve endings were singing, her body flooding with liquid heat. She lifted her arms and pulled the bra off first one side and then the other before letting it fall to the floor behind her.

She felt the heat of a blush rising up her neck, but she refused to acknowledge it. Instead, she tilted her chin up and put her hands on her hips, daring him to look his fill.

She didn't know what to expect next, but Jack clearly did.

"That's it," he said. "I forfeit."

Shoving the cards aside, he reached for her. Panic threaded through her, but she shoved it down deep and went into his arms. How could she deny that it was where she wanted to be? Where she'd known she would end up almost from the first moment she'd met him?

He stroked the skin of her shoulder, his fingers so gentle and light that she shivered, little goose bumps rising in the wake of his touch.

"You are amazingly beautiful," he said before his mouth came down on hers.

Her first thought was that if she wanted to preserve herself, preserve her heart, then she needed to push him away.

Her second was that she couldn't stop this thing between them from running its course. The tension had been unbearable for days now, tightening as they played this game, and this was the only form of release that would be acceptable to them both. Whatever happened, she was so entangled now that she could do nothing but enjoy the ride.

She wanted him inside her, on top of her, tangled up with her, loving her with the fierceness and ruthlessness that were the hallmarks of his personality.

She wanted him, all of him. Desperately.

Cara speared her fingers into his hair, loving the texture. She finally felt free to touch, to explore, to claim him as her own. With the loss of her bra, everything had changed. They'd crossed a line over which there could be no retreat. The only way out was forward.

Jack urged her closer until she was sitting with her legs on either side of him. Then he put his broad hands on her bottom and pulled her against the ridge of his erection.

Cara gasped as sensation streaked through her at the simple contact of their bodies through the thin fabric separating them. It had been a long time since she'd been with a man. She hadn't realized how much she missed this kind of contact. Except that everything with Jack seemed to feel so much more intense than it ever had with anyone else.

He flexed his hips, pressing hard into her center, and her body responded with a surge of moisture. The kiss deepened, their tongues tangling with an urgency she'd never experienced before. The kiss was hot, intense, and deep—but it wasn't enough.

She tried to get closer, couldn't stop the moan that vibrated in her throat.

Jack immediately broke the kiss, leaving her empty and disappointed. "I forgot about your lip. I'm sorry."

"No," she said, "that's not it at all. Kiss me, Jack. Don't stop kissing me."

He fused his mouth to hers again. And then he

was lifting her, pushing her back onto the bed, coming down on top of her. His body was big and hard, and she loved the feel of him pressing into her.

When his hand closed over the slope of her breast, she arched her back, thrusting into his hand. He pinched her nipple, softly, expertly, until she was a quivering mass of sensitive nerve endings.

"Jack," she said, her voice breathy and thick. Tears pressed against the backs of her eyes. Tears of joy, of frustration, of unimaginable sorrow. She didn't know why she felt all these things with him, but the intensity of it physically hurt.

"I know," he replied before kissing his way down her neck, over her collarbone. His fingers shaped her ribs, the slope of her breast, the soft skin of her abdomen. She couldn't pull herself away now even if she wanted to.

And she definitely didn't want to.

The moment his mouth closed over her nipple, she cried out. The pleasure was so intense, so unbelievably intense, as he sucked the hard, tight bud between his lips. Her fingers clutched in his hair, on his shoulders.

He slid a hand down her abdomen, beneath the silk of her panties, found the hot, wet center of her body. He groaned as his fingers sank between her legs.

Those fingers, those clever fingers that handled the cards so expertly, began to play her body like a fine instrument. Two fingers pinched and kneaded her clitoris, making her cry out with the pleasure. And then he was dipping lower, inserting a finger into her body, joining it with a second one as his thumb took up the rhythm above.

His mouth played her nipples while his fingers stroked her—and Cara came unglued at the seams. Her body tightened painfully, so very painfully, as she flexed her hips and tried to make his hand move faster.

She could feel the release gathering, feel it coming, feel every cell of her body vibrate with energy and need—

And then it happened. She reached the peak and fell off the other side, sobbing and gasping the whole way.

CHAPTER NINE

JACK had never felt this kind of urgency before. When he made love to a woman, he took his time. He was in control, always in supreme control.

But not this time. Cara's breathy little moans, the way she curled her fingers into his skin, the sweet intensity of her voice as she shattered beneath his fingertips—not to mention the hot, wet feel of her, the way she sizzled and shook, the scent of her skin—he had to have her.

Right now.

His side hurt, but he didn't care. He'd never felt such sweet pain as the pain of his arousal. His injuries simply didn't compare.

Cara was still shaking from the power of her release as he practically tore the silk panties from her body. Then he was shoving off his underwear and settling between her legs again. She opened to him immediately, her long legs wrapping around his hips as he pushed inside.

He had no finesse. None whatsoever. He'd lost

it somewhere along the way. Cara was ready for him, more than ready, but she gasped a little at his possession, her chest rising and falling rapidly as she waited for her body to accommodate him.

But he couldn't speak, couldn't ask her if she was okay, because it took every ounce of control he had not to take her hard and fast. His body urged him to cast off restraint, to use her sweet lushness for his pleasure, to spend himself wildly in frenzied lovemaking.

He held himself rigidly, fighting for control— and then she reached up with a soft hand, stroked it across his cheek.

"Jack," she said softly. "Oh, Jack."

Tears glazed her eyes, but he understood instinctively that they weren't tears of pain or unhappiness. My God, she was beautiful. And she was *his*.

Just like that, he lost whatever tenuous grip on his sanity that he'd had. He began to move, relentless, stroking into her body. He rode her hard, but she met him all the way, her lush body tilting up to his, her hips opening to him, her lovely breasts bouncing with the force of their lovemaking.

It drove him insane. She drove him insane. He held on as long as he could, held on to the tight knot of pleasure gathering at the base of his spine until he felt her body tighten around him. A moment later and she was arching her back, thrusting her breasts up, gasping as her climax hit her. He sucked one of her nipples into his mouth, gloried in the sharpening of her cry as he increased her pleasure.

She was so incredibly responsive. When she collapsed on the bed again, he grasped her buttocks and lifted her to him, angling her until her body began to spark once more. It didn't take much to make her come again.

This time when she went over the edge, he went with her, spilling his body into hers with such force that his vision went black for a split second. It was the most amazing, most wonderful feeling to find his release in Cara's lush body.

But at the back of his mind, dampening the sensual afterglow, was the knowledge it wouldn't last. It never did. Nothing ever kept his attention longer than it took to establish his dominance. Not even a woman as sweetly sexy as Cara Taylor.

Cara awoke to the sounds of the shower running. Pushing herself up in the plush bed, she blinked and yawned—and then it hit her. Where she was. Who she was with.

What she'd done.

Oh, God.

Her body was pleasurably languid, though she acknowledged the slight soreness between her legs, as well. Her heart skipped a beat. They'd made love endlessly, it seemed. Sleeping, waking to tangle themselves together on the crisp, cool sheets, sleeping again, waking to make love once more.

She'd never had a lover like Jack, a man who was so attuned to her body that he could make her crave him with the slightest touch. It was so dangerous, this feeling she had when she was with him. She could love him if she wasn't careful.

Cara sat up and wrapped her arms around her knees.

No. She would not go there. She was a grown woman, in control of her destiny and her body. She'd made love with Jack—had *sex* with Jack, she corrected—because she had needs and because he was mighty good at fulfilling them.

Women could have sex for the sake of sex, too. She'd just done so. Over and over again.

Cara tucked a lock of hair behind her ear and told herself to stop blushing. She could feel the heat in her skin, could feel the warmth creeping up her spine, her neck, over her cheeks.

What the hell was there to blush about?

She whipped the covers back and stood, stretched. She went over to the huge walk-in closet, where all her things had been hung up when they'd first arrived. A full-length mirror sat at the back of the dressing area, and Cara jolted to a stop. Who was that woman?

Her naked body glowed. Her skin was luminous, her long hair a wild tangle down her back. Her green eyes were slumberous. She looked tousled and satiated, as if she'd been having sex for hours—which, she acknowledged, she had.

Her breasts were full and firm, the deep pink nipples budded tight in anticipation of her lover's touch. There were red marks on her shoulder, her neck, even her abdomen, where Jack's stubble had abraded her tender skin.

The marks on her abdomen stole her breath as she thought of how they'd gotten there. He'd kissed and licked his way down her body, spread her legs open and then taken her to heaven with his tongue.

Cara bit her lip at the memory. If Jack came out of the bathroom and wanted to do everything all over again, she'd jump at the chance.

Instead, she found a robe and belted it around her body. Then she selected undergarments and headed for the bath. Jack was standing at the mirror with a towel draped low around his lean hips, razor in hand.

He stopped when she walked in and turned to look at her. She didn't know what to say to him after last night. She felt awkward, out of place, and it angered her. Because she hadn't felt that way before they'd slept together. She'd known she needed to keep her distance from him, but she hadn't done it.

Jack reached for her, pulled her against his damp, warm body. He smelled fresh and clean from the shower as he dipped to kiss her.

She opened her mouth beneath his, surprised with how much she still wanted him. She could feel him hardening, his penis pressing insistently against her thigh. She reached beneath the towel and took him in her hand. His velvety skin was hot. She squeezed ever so lightly.

Jack groaned. A moment later he was shoving the robe from her body, licking his way to her nipples while she threw her head back and moaned.

"I want you to see us, to see what you do to me," he said roughly, turning her until she faced the mirror. She was almost as tall as he was, but his body dwarfed hers. He was all lean, tanned muscle—and he quite simply took her breath away.

He clasped her breasts, his fingers tweaking her nipples, pinching and pulling them until she thought she would come apart simply from his touch. In the light of the bathroom, his tanned skin looked so stark against her creamy complexion. The contrast made her shiver.

"You're beautiful, Cara," he said in her ear, his breath sending pleasurable vibrations over her sensitive skin. "I want you again."

"Yes," she breathed.

She thought he would turn her to face him, would grab her hand and haul her back to the bed. But he didn't. Instead, he bent her over and gripped her hips.

Cara gasped. It was so erotic, what he was about to do. So raw. She wasn't a stranger to varied love-making—and yet she didn't think she could survive something so private, so sensual, as watching this man make love to her in the mirror.

But she didn't want to stop it. She wanted him again, desperately. She wanted to see his face, wanted to see her own, even though it frightened her. What would she see in her own eyes while he took her?

As he slid inside her body, their eyes locked in the mirror. Cara gasped again with the fullness of his possession—it was slightly different from his angle—but she didn't want him to stop. She gripped the edge of the counter as he began to move. Their gazes remained tangled, as if it were a contest to see who could last the longest without looking away.

It was Jack who closed his eyes first. His head tilted back, and the look of sheer ecstasy on his face made her heart squeeze tight in her chest.

A moment later, his fingers found her clitoris and she could no longer concentrate on watching him. She could only feel, could only see the bigger picture of the two of them together, could only marvel at the sensations streaking through her and the shameless way she enjoyed everything he did to her.

They didn't last long. Cara shattered within moments and Jack followed immediately after. She leaned on her elbows, breathing hard. It should have felt impersonal, the way they'd just had sex, but nothing could be farther from the truth. She felt as if their souls had twined, as if they'd seen a part of each other that no one ever had before.

In the next moment, she chided herself for being silly. Jack was highly sensual. He'd made love to many women. She was just the flavor of the week.

He disengaged from her body and she felt bereft with the loss of him. But then he turned on the shower and led her under the spray.

They didn't come out for a very long time.

That afternoon, they checked out of the hotel. Cara thought they would return to Paris, but instead Jack took her to a grand apartment overlooking the Thames and the London skyline. Like his Paris apartment, this one was furnished in sleek, modern lines. Unlike the Paris apartment, this building was as modern as the furnishings.

"Why did we stay in the hotel last night when this is so close?" she asked as she scanned the view. There were the Houses of Parliament, Big Ben…and so many other things she couldn't even identify.

Jack turned from his perusal of a stack of mail. "It seemed like the thing to do at the time."

Cara frowned as she watched him go through the mail. What had happened between them had been amazing—too amazing, if she were honest with herself. Because now she didn't want to do what she needed to do: she didn't want to ask him for the money so she could get back to her own life.

"Is there any word on my passport and bank card?" she asked.

He looked up again. "I have someone working on it. But no, not yet."

"You realize I can't go home until I have my passport back." There, she'd said it. She'd voiced her fear and given him a hint of what she intended. If he couldn't get her passport for her, she would go to the American embassy and apply for a new one. She wasn't worried about anyone using her bank card—they'd need her PIN to do so—but if she didn't get that back soon, she'd report it missing and get a new one sent to her here in London.

He tossed the mail aside and gave her a heated look that curled her toes. How did he manage that when they'd made love only a few hours ago now?

"In a hurry to leave me, Cara?"

"I've completed my end of the bargain," she said, her heart pumping hard and fast.

The heat in his eyes banked. "You'll get your money. And your passport as soon as I have it."

She suddenly felt as if she'd made a mistake. She wanted to go to him, wanted to put her arms around his waist and press her cheek to his chest. She wanted to tell him she was sorry, that she wasn't trying to rush away, but that she had to do it for her own good.

Because she cared about him. Too much. In so very short a time, Jack Wolfe had managed to worm his way beneath her defenses and make her care.

But she knew she couldn't trust him. Couldn't give him her heart. It never worked out, that kind of blind trust. Her mother had had it with her father, and look where it had gotten her. Brokenhearted and broke. Cara wouldn't suffer the same fate. Jack was gorgeous and amazing in bed, but that was the extent of it. She *wouldn't* love him.

She believed in happy ever after, but she knew that kind of love wasn't one-sided. It couldn't be. And there was absolutely nothing about Jack that said he was in danger of falling in love with her.

"This isn't going anywhere, Jack," she said. "You and I both know it."

He looked so dark and furious. "We've spent one night together. It's a little soon to be thinking about the future, isn't it?"

"Maybe for you," she said, stung. "But I have to find another job and get on with my life. I can't stay here as your—what? Paid companion?"

"That part is over," he said, his voice measured. "I paid you to go to the wedding. You went. We've moved on now."

"To what?"

His jaw flexed. "I have work to do," he said. "If you need anything, I'll be in my office. It's down the hall, on the left."

"Is this usually how you end your discussions?" she asked. "By walking away?"

He turned back to her. "What discussion, Cara? You've said you want to leave. I've said I'm working on it."

"You don't let anyone in, do you?"

Surprise flashed across his face. A moment later, he was as cool and unflappable as always. "As I said, I'll be in my office."

Cara stood with her arms wrapped around her middle as she watched him go. She was furious, and yet there was nothing left to say, was there? Angry tears pressed against the backs of her eyes.

She refused to let them fall. Crying over a man was weakness, even if she was crying in anger.

She was not weak. She would never be weak. The sooner she got control of her life back and got out of here, the better.

Jack spent the afternoon on the computer. The markets in New York had just opened; it was exactly what he needed to lose himself for a while.

He bought and sold thousands of shares, knowing just when to begin and end each transaction. The thrill of the chase was always exhilarating, always got his blood pumping and his adrenaline firing along all his synapses.

But it was different this time. Different because he couldn't completely stop thinking about the woman in the other room. She'd accused him of shutting her out, of shutting everyone out.

He'd wanted to deny it, and yet he couldn't. Because relationships were unpredictable at best. If you couldn't count on the people you shared DNA with to be there for you, how could you ever rely on another person? Knowing that had saved him a lot of angst over the years.

Jack clicked another button. His game was still sharp, and he made money as always, but he wanted to stop, wanted to go and haul Cara against him. Wanted to strip her naked and lose himself in her delightful body again.

It was odd, this feeling. He was a highly sexual man, and he enjoyed making love to the women he dated—but he'd never quite been this obsessed with one. It was a shock to want her again so badly within moments of finding his release in her body. Sex was a pleasurable pursuit, but it wasn't an addiction.

Until Cara.

He was getting hard just thinking about her. He shoved thoughts of her aside ruthlessly, clicked on a "Buy" button. The transaction went through, but instead of feeling the elation he usually felt, he was frustrated.

Frustrated because he wanted to be with Cara. Wanted those legs wrapped around him while he thrust into her beautiful body. But more than that, he wanted to talk to her. He'd enjoyed talking to her before they'd lost control with each other, and he found that he wanted to talk to her almost as much as he wanted to make love to her.

He *liked* her.

Jack focused on the computer screen. She only cared about her money, and about leaving, so why was he thinking of her so much? There was nothing between them except great sex. And he could enjoy that for the next few days with her—assuming she was still speaking to him. He clicked a "Sell" button, his blood humming with anticipation as he watched the money pile up in his account.

By the time he finished his transactions, it was after eight o'clock. Jack shoved back from the computer. He'd forced himself to concentrate, and he'd made money, but this restless hunger gnawing beneath the surface had grown stronger with the passing hours.

He found Cara on the balcony off the living room. Below, the city stretched out in a never-ending carpet of light and sound. Car horns and screeching tires filtered up from far below. Cara leaned against the railing, cradling a wineglass in one hand. She took a sip and returned her attention to the sights.

She still wore the sea-green sleeveless dress she'd had on earlier, but she'd taken off the heels she'd been wearing. She had one bare foot propped on the railing, the other flat on the polished stone of the balcony.

"Are you hungry?" he asked.

She spun around, her hand over her heart. "My word, Jack Wolfe, you scared the living daylights out of me."

He loved her accent, especially when she got a little flustered. It was Southern, but there was a hint of something else, as well. The Cajun in her, he supposed. He'd listened to her speaking French in Paris and marveled at the sensual way she said the words, the thickness of them on her tongue. It was different, earthier, than the French he was used to. It called up thoughts of dark, sultry nights. Silk sheets, sweat and incense. He wanted to know her, wanted to know what had made her into this infuriatingly sexy and independent woman. He wanted, he acknowledged to himself, to own her...body and soul.

"What were you thinking about so intently?" As if he didn't know. He didn't regret walking away from her earlier, but he regretted not telling her he wanted her to stay because he liked being with her.

She tucked a long lock of hair behind her ear. "A lot, actually."

He moved onto the balcony to join her, took the glass from her. She willingly handed it over and he took a sip before giving it back. He refused to think about the intimacy of the gesture, the ease with which he could get used to this.

"Like what?" he pressed.

She sighed. "Home. Mama. You."

You. That gratified him. "What about me?"

Her eyes were warm and smooth, like green onyx. She studied him carefully. He got the impression she was trying to decide how to answer. He wasn't sure if that was a good thing or a bad thing, but it was too late to take back the question.

"I was thinking that I hardly know you. And that I wish I could've applied the brakes to this thing between us and backed up a few steps before last night."

"Fast can be good. Sometimes you have to live life on the edge, Cara."

"I'm not much good at living life on the edge."

Jack shrugged. "Actually, I'd say you're quite good at it."

She shook her head adamantly. "No, really, I'm not. This…*whatever* this is with us…has skipped a lot of steps for me."

He could tell that she was genuinely stressed by it, but it was too late for regrets. He had no intention of stepping back now. He needed her too much.

Needed? It was a strong word, and not one he typically used, but he couldn't think of a better one at the moment. And he had every intention of pressing his advantage. Because she wanted him, no matter what she said about this thing between them going nowhere.

Besides, to bed was somewhere—and that's where he intended to take her.

"What do you suggest?" he asked, taking the glass from her and sipping again.

She watched him drink. He wondered if she knew the hunger that was in her eyes, the answering hunger she called up in him.

And yet he knew she wasn't about to suggest they take this into the bedroom. He got the impression she was fighting herself very hard not to give in to her physical urges. He would let her do so, for now. But she would be his tonight, and every night so long as they were together.

He pushed aside thoughts of her passport, thoughts of her walking out of his life. It didn't bother him, not really. He simply wasn't ready for this to end quite yet. And he didn't think she was, either, no matter what she'd said earlier.

She licked her lips, and his body turned to stone. "I think we should talk."

"Fine," he replied.

He expected the usual female chatter about feelings and plans for the future. He hadn't handled it well earlier, when he was still feeling raw and exposed, but he could do it. He knew enough about this kind of talk to navigate it fairly well. She would want to know about his childhood—he wouldn't tell her the truth of that, but he did have a prepared answer he usually gave. She'd want to know about his past loves, his goals and dreams and plans.

He knew what to say in response to those things. He'd done it before, many times. And when she was satisfied, he'd ask her the same questions. He was even looking forward to the answers.

But what she said was not at all what he expected to hear.

"Then tell me what happened yesterday in the bar."

CHAPTER TEN

JACK'S gaze, which had been so full of heat and sexual promise that she'd had a hard time concentrating on what she wanted to say, had gone utterly cold.

But she didn't regret asking, dammit. In spite of what had happened earlier, she wanted to know where she stood with him. She'd had enough time to cool off and think. He'd pushed her away because he didn't want to let anyone in. And though it might be the smart thing to just wash her hands of him entirely, she couldn't quite do it yet.

But this was the line in the sand. If he brushed her off, then she knew exactly what he thought of her. Of them.

He took another long draft of her wine, then handed the glass back to her. "It's a long story."

"I have time."

"Here's the condensed version," he said, his words sounding as if he'd bitten them off. "Jacob left home when we needed him most. Lucas had to step up and be man of the house. But he couldn't handle it, either, so he left, too. And then there was me. I didn't run away."

Cara's heart was hammering inside her breast-bone. She hadn't expected this much from him, she really hadn't. She'd been prepared to walk away, knowing she'd done her best. But he'd just thrown her a curveball.

"I'm sorry," she said softly. It wasn't the whole story, she was certain, and yet she could feel his pain as if it were her own. She knew about taking on responsibility that you didn't think you were ready for. About unfairness and duty.

"I was seventeen," he said bitterly. "And I had to take care of four younger siblings the best I could. It was Jacob's duty to be there for us. But he couldn't do it. He couldn't handle the pressure."

"But you could."

"Yes."

"You might not believe this, Jack, but I understand the way you feel. Katrina changed a lot of things in my life. It's not the same thing, I know, but I do understand the feeling of being trapped by doing what's right."

His eyes gleamed with anger and bitterness. "You can never understand what I've been through, Cara. Be grateful for that."

"I've had to sacrifice things—"

"That's not what I'm talking about."

"All right. Then tell me."

"I—" He shoved a hand through his hair. "Dammit."

She reached for his hand, squeezed. "It's okay, ack."

"It's ugly. You have no idea…"

Cara bit her lip. She wanted to know, and she didn't. The anguish on his face disconcerted her, made her search for something less difficult to talk about. "What do you think your brother wanted to say to you?"

She'd seen the way Jacob had looked at Jack yesterday. He'd seemed…remorseful. As if he'd wanted to say something important, but Jack had exploded and shut him down before he could do t.

Jack opened his mouth. Closed it again, his expression turning to granite. "I don't know. I don't care."

Then he reached for her, pulled her into his arms and nuzzled the skin of her neck. A thrill went through her, and a twinge of sadness, as well. He'd tried, but he didn't really want to be close to her in any way other than physically. Sex was what he wanted. No doubt he'd been humoring her in order to get to that point.

Cara put her palms on his chest. His skin burned her through the fabric of the casual cotton polo he wore. So hot, always so hot. She licked her lips, her throat suddenly as dry as a desert.

She had a choice. She could pretend none of this had happened, pretend she wasn't hurt by his unwillingness to share more with her—or she could go to bed alone. It wasn't an easy choice, but she had to stand up for herself. She wasn't simply his sex toy. She wasn't here just to fulfill his physical needs. She was worth more than that. If not to him, then at least to herself.

His mouth was magical where it skimmed along her throat. Another few moments, and she'd never be able to say no. Cara's fists curled into his shirt.

"I'm tired, Jack. It's been a long few days."

He stiffened. She wasn't sure what he would do, what he would say, but he let her go and stepped back. His eyes were pewter in the evening light. Already, she was regretting that she'd pushed him away. She wanted to press a kiss to his hard jaw, wanted him to soften and smile again. But she wouldn't do it. Not tonight, not with her heart breaking like this.

"Then I'll say good-night," he said. She waited for him to say something else, prayed he would say something else, but he didn't. He left her standing alone on the balcony with the night sounds of London ringing in her ears.

* * *

What had Jacob wanted? That was the billion-dollar question so far as Jack was concerned. There was nothing Jacob could say that would ever erase the pain and anger of his abandonment. So why was Jack now wondering what his brother wanted?

And why was he thinking of Cara and the way she'd looked at him when he'd told her he didn't know and didn't care?

Damn her for making him wonder! Damn her for making him question his own reaction. He hadn't been able to control the rage that had burst from him at the sight of his brother, of that face he'd once loved and admired so much. He'd felt every sick moment of Jacob's betrayal then. The panic and fear when they'd discovered that Jacob was gone, that all he'd left was a note and that he wasn't coming back again.

It had hurt so much back then. He'd thought he was over it, but the moment he'd seen Jacob again, everything inside him had boiled over.

How could he explain it to Cara? Why would he want to? This thing with Jacob had nothing to do with the two of them. He resented her for making it into an issue between them. He didn't want her to know about the ugliness of his life before, didn't want to have to see her pitying expression when he told her about it.

Jack threw down the pen he was holding and put

his head in his hands. It was two in the morning and he was still thinking about this. Still thinking about *her*. He wanted to go to her, wanted to explain why he couldn't talk about this.

But why should he have to do that at all? What happened years ago had nothing to do with right now.

Goddammit. He wasn't doing this. He wasn't sitting here and beating himself up over it. It was his life and he'd do what he damn well wanted. What he'd always done.

Jack tapped a key on his computer, brought up the Japanese markets. They were already well into the trading day, but that wouldn't stop him from making a killing before it was over.

When Cara awoke, light was streaming through the shades and across the bed where she lay. She turned her head. She was alone. Jack's side of the bed hadn't even been slept in. Guilt shafted through her. Had he slept on the couch? Slept in his office?

Or had he left during the night?

Cara flipped the covers back and grabbed her robe. He wouldn't dare leave her alone here would he? She didn't know why, but panic unwound inside her at the thought. She didn't pause to analyze it.

She burst from the bedroom and hurried through

the vast apartment. He wasn't in the kitchen, the living room or on the balcony that ran the length of the apartment. She stopped, straining to hear any sound—and realized he was in his office. She could hear the clackety-clack of a keyboard as she got closer. Pushing the door open, she stopped and watched him.

"Have you slept at all?" she said, her voice rusty.

His head snapped up. And then he turned to look at the skyline outside his window, as if he'd only just realized it was broad daylight. Another click of the keys and then he was pushing back from the computer.

"I lost track of time," he said, as if it made perfect sense that he would do so.

"So you've been at the computer all night?"

"Technically, I suppose so. But it's the end of the trading day in Asia."

"Trading," she repeated. He was up all night trading? Trading what? Not baseball cards, surely. As if a British man would be interested in baseball, she thought.

The shadow of his beard had grown into a day's worth of stubble. Why did he look so unbearably sexy unshaven? And why did she want to go over and pull his head down to hers, kiss him until neither one of them could breathe?

Stocks. The word popped into her head, and she

felt silly for not thinking of it sooner. Jack owned an investment firm. He'd told her that, and yet she kept seeing him as this maverick card shark, this daredevil who lived life on the edge.

Though perhaps trading stocks was a bit daredevilish.

"Did you make any money?" she asked.

He smiled. He didn't look in the least bit weary. If not for his rumpled clothing and day's growth of beard, she wouldn't know he'd been up all night.

"A killing," he said. "As usual."

He had a knack for making money, no doubt about it. "I'm sure your clients appreciate your ability," she said softly.

"They do. But I wasn't using the firm's money."

Just as she'd thought, he risked everything on the vagaries of the market. Chance was Jack's constant companion. She didn't understand how he could stomach the uncertainty. But then, that was Jack.

"Then I guess it's good you won."

"It will be for a lot of people."

Cara shook her head. "I don't understand."

Jack shoved his hands in his pockets, almost as if he were embarrassed somehow. "I don't need the money," he said. "I like to use it where it'll do the most good."

Cara's heart was thundering for an entirely

different reason now. "You're giving money to charity?"

His brows drew down as he studied her. "You seem surprised."

"No, not at all," she hastened to reassure him. But she was surprised, and it shamed her. Why had she thought he only cared for himself? That he was irresponsible with money and unaware of how lucky he was to have so much of it? She should have known better. The man who'd charged in—at great risk to himself—because he'd thought she needed rescuing was not the sort of man who would turn a blind eye to the suffering of others.

Jack shrugged as he shoved a hand through his hair. "No, it's all right. I understand. I've given you little reason to think otherwise, have I?"

Cara hugged her body as the heat of a blush flooded her. "I think I said before that we don't really know each other very well. Everything has been backward."

"Maybe we should work on that."

Happiness was a tangible force inside her. "Do you mean it, Jack?"

He reached out and stroked two fingers along her cheek, her jaw, down her throat. She shivered with the contact. How did he do this to her? How did he make her want to forget everything she'd ever learned about relying only on herself?

"I want to make love to you, Cara. But I want

to know you, too. I want to know what makes you the way you are."

"The way I am?"

"Fierce. Independent. Unwilling to accept help when you need it."

"I didn't need your help," she said, knowing instinctively that he was talking about the night in the casino. "You made everything worse by coming after me."

He snorted. "You don't still believe that fiction, do you? Bobby Gold isn't a nice man, Cara. And you cost him fifteen million euros."

She thrust her chin up. She didn't want to admit that he had a point, because to do so would be to admit that maybe she wasn't as in control as she liked to think. She was so used to taking care of herself, taking care of her family, that she'd never considered she wouldn't manage in that situation. But what if she hadn't? What if Bobby had decided to use her as an example for his other employees? If she'd disappeared in a foreign country, how long would it have taken for anyone to notice? It wasn't like she was a tourist, or that she called Mama every night.

"Fine," Cara admitted. "Maybe I didn't have it under control. But I didn't really cost him fifteen million. He kept it, remember? And he'd have found a way to do so regardless of whether or not you followed me. You'd have never made it out of the casino with the money. And you know it."

He was glowering at her, but then he suddenly grinned. It was as if a summer thunderstorm had unexpectedly broke apart and let the sun shine down. "Then maybe we helped each other, hmm?"

"Maybe so."

"Are you hungry?" he asked.

Cara nodded.

"Get dressed and we'll go out for breakfast."

"But aren't you tired?" she asked incredulously.

"I'll sleep later."

Cara showered and dressed in a pair of tan slacks and a pearl knit top. Jack was waiting for her when she emerged from the bedroom. He'd also showered and changed, and his face was freshly shaven. He looked happier this morning, as if a good night's sleep had done wonders for him.

Except that he hadn't slept. Cara frowned, but he showed no signs of slowing down. Instead of hailing a cab, they walked the short distance to a café he swore had the best coffee in all of London. Over a meal of bacon, eggs, toast, grilled tomatoes and coffee, they talked about mundane things like the temperature and the clear sky. It seemed odd after their charged evening, but Cara decided to just enjoy it for the moment.

She liked talking to him, even if it was about nothing.

"Tell me about you," Jack said after she'd commented on a woman and her dog in the small park across the street. The dog was wearing a pink dress with a ruffle, which Cara found hilarious.

She swung around to look at him. "Dogs don't wear pink dresses where I come from," she said with a smile.

Jack's silvery gaze was piercing, as if he'd wanted more from her than that. "It's a crime against nature," he agreed. He reached for her hand, threaded his fingers through hers—and she knew she'd been right. "But that's not what I want to know."

Her heart began to flutter. "What *do* you want to know?"

"Why you think you have to do everything yourself. Why you don't want to accept help from anyone."

Cara swallowed. "I can accept help. I'm just used to taking care of myself."

"But why? What happened to you that you have such a strong need to be independent?"

Her skin prickled with heat. "Who said anything happened? I prefer relying on myself, is all. I wasn't born with a silver spoon in my mouth."

"Like I was, right?" His voice was a little harder, a little flatter.

"I didn't say that at all." She hadn't even thought it when she'd spoken, but she understood how he could see it as a dig at him. She'd just meant that she'd always known what it was to work, whether it was watching her parents do so or getting her first job as a cashier when she was sixteen.

"This is supposed to be about you," he said, as if he were accusing her of trying to turn the conversation.

And maybe she was, she admitted. But conversation was a two-way street. Give a little, get a little.

"No," she said. "It's supposed to be about us getting to know each other better."

He let go of her hand and leaned back against his seat, his eyes hard. She didn't feel like she'd won a victory. Instead, she felt as if she'd taken a wrong turn on a dark road.

"Fine," he said, his voice clipped. "I was indeed born rich. It was a bit of a chaotic childhood, however."

"Because your mother died and you hated your father," she said softly, annoyed now that she'd pushed him down this path.

"My father was a tyrant," he snapped out. "A beast with a temper. You asked how I could tell my ribs were bruised and not broken. I learned it from my father."

Her heart constricted at the thought of him cowering from his father's rage. What kind of man could beat children so severely? For all her father's faults, he'd never been violent. A liar, yes. Violent, no.

"I'm so sorry, Jack."

He looked murderously angry. His eyes burned so hot they seared her. But this time the heat wasn't good. It wasn't the flame of desire and passion, but the frozen burn of despair and pain.

She hurt so much for him she physically ached. And she suddenly knew she didn't need him to say another word. "You don't have to—"

"Yes, I hated him," he bit out. "If I'd been the one who killed him, I wouldn't have run away." He leaned forward, his eyes still burning. "He scarred Annabelle for life, Cara. He beat her so severely with a whip that she almost died."

Tears filled her eyes. She couldn't stop one from escaping and slipping down her cheek.

Jack's gaze hardened, but he didn't cease talking. "Jacob tried to stop him. He fell and hit his head and died instantly. It was an accident." He sucked in a breath as his fingers clenched into a fist on the table. "But you know the worst part, Cara? I'd have gladly killed him myself if I'd been there instead of Jacob."

"Don't say that, Jack—"

He shoved away from the table and stood. He was breathing hard now, as if he'd fought his way through a jungle. She imagined that he had. A jungle of dark memories and bitter emotions that he couldn't escape no matter how he tried.

"*No*. That's the kind of man I am, Cara. You wanted to know the truth about me. Now you've got it."

CHAPTER ELEVEN

She let him hide out in his office for several hours before she decided enough was enough. Cara put down the book she'd been reading—she wasn't doing a very good job of distracting herself anyway—and marched down the hall to Jack's office. She could hear him behind the door, hear the clicking of the keys and the smooth timbre of his voice as he spoke to someone on the phone. She pressed a hand to the door and just listened.

He'd been awake for hours now, working nonstop, and she was worried about him. After his confession at breakfast, they'd returned to the apartment. He'd gone out for a while—on business, he'd said—but when he'd returned, he'd retreated to his office with hardly a word.

She'd wanted to give him his space. He'd pushed her away earlier; perhaps he thought he'd pushed her away for good with that confession about his father, but it was time she disabused him of the notion.

She hurt for him so much. If she could, she would take his pain way. It had horrified her when he'd said he'd have killed his father if he could have, but she understood where that kind of emotion came from. She'd never wanted to kill her father, but she'd been so angry with him for what he'd done. It had taken months to explain it to Remy, who only knew that his routine had been upset. He didn't understand why Daddy was gone, had cried and screamed endlessly when Daddy didn't come home as expected.

Cara shuddered with the memory. Then she gathered herself and pushed open the door. No knocking, because she wouldn't give him the chance to rebuff her.

He looked up as she entered. He was still on the phone, but she didn't care. She knew enough about Jack to know he always got what he wanted when it came to money. If the call were important, he'd find another way to complete the transaction later.

He looked so starkly handsome behind his desk, with the city spread out behind him. She walked over to the windows and calmly closed the blinds. Jack's eyes followed her, but he still hadn't put down the phone.

Cara began to unbutton the long sheath dress she'd put on this morning. Buttons ran down the entire front of the formfitting black cotton.

"Yes," Jack said to the person on the other end of the line. But his eyes were glued to her. Cara smiled wickedly as she peeled the first part of the dress open to reveal the red lacy bra she'd put on beneath it.

"Um, whatever you say."

Cara unbuttoned the dress enough to step out of it. Then she turned around and laid it over a chair, knowing he would get an eyeful because of the matching red thong she'd worn.

"No, no. Nothing's wrong," he said, but his voice sounded strained. "Look, can I call you back?"

Turning, she marched over to him, reaching him right as he hung up the phone. She didn't give him a chance to say a thing before she pushed his chair back and straddled him. Gripping his face in her hands, she tilted his head back and crushed her mouth down on his.

Their lovemaking was not in the least bit tame. Cara tore at his clothes as he filled his hands with her breasts. He pulled the cups down and tweaked her nipples into tight points while she kissed him. Then he slipped a finger beneath the lace of her panty and began stroking her in that most sensitive of places. Cara shuddered and ground her hips against him.

But as much as she wanted to let him bring her to fulfillment, she wanted to take care of him first. This was about him, about how much she wanted him to understand that nothing he could ever tell her about himself would scare her away.

She shoved his shirt off his shoulders, then started to unbutton his pants. The instant she'd unzipped him, she slipped down his body and took him in her mouth.

"Cara," he gasped as she swirled her tongue around his hot shaft. She loved the size of him, the feel, the way he bucked against her tongue. It turned her on to know she was doing this to him, that he was fisting his hands in her hair and groaning because of the way she made him feel.

But before she could bring him to completion, he pushed her away.

"Inside you," he said, standing and lifting her onto his desk. Another moment and she was clinging to him as he thrust into her body.

Everything about the way they made love was intense. Cara's head fell back as pleasure and emotion overwhelmed her. Was that her voice moaning and pleading for more? It shocked her, and yet she shouldn't be surprised. She loved what they did to each other, loved the way he made her feel, and she'd missed this last night much more than she'd have thought possible.

They exploded together, gasping and grinding into each other for that last little bit of bliss, before collapsing on the desk in a boneless heap.

Sometime later, they made their way into the bed room and made love again, slowly this time, with more control and more focus on making the pleasure last as long as possible.

Cara fell asleep in his arms, her body temporarily sated of her craving for him. When she awoke he was gone. She sat up, disappointed. Had he gone back to his computer? They'd never spoken a word, other than those of hunger and need and pleasure.

And speaking of hunger, she smelled something cooking. Cara got out of bed and slipped into her robe.

Jack was at the stove. The smells of oil and garlic and tomatoes wafted up from the pan he was tending. He tossed in a handful of mushrooms and stirred. She took a moment to watch him, to marvel at the sight of an unbelievably sexy man moving around a kitchen like he knew what he was doing.

"It smells good," she said.

He turned. "I thought you might be hungry."

She leaned against the center island and watched him work. "I'm starved. What are you making?"

"It's just pasta with a few fresh ingredients."

"Wow, I'd have thought you had someone do your cooking for you."

He didn't turn back to her as he shook his

head. "Not usually, no. I don't like the intrusion of having someone around."

Her heart flipped at that statement. Was she an intrusion, too? Or, if not now, would she soon become one?

He finished the sauce and drained the pasta, then plated the food and set it on the bar. Cara climbed on the bar stool and twirled her fork in the pasta.

"It's good," she said after she'd had the first bite.

He was watching her eat, and she dipped her head again, embarrassed. Odd, considering how they had no secrets when it came to making love. He'd certainly seen more unguarded expressions on her face, had heard her make intimate noises in the throes of passion.

"I'm sorry about earlier," he said.

Cara looked up. "What's there to be sorry about?"

"I shouldn't have said what I did."

She dropped her fork and reached for his hand. "No, Jack, don't apologize for that. I don't blame you for feeling that way."

"I don't usually talk about it. In fact, I think you're only the second person to ever hear me say it."

Her heart quickened. "I'm glad you felt like you could tell me."

He blew out a breath and looked away. "It's so ugly, Cara. Everything that happened, everything I felt—"

He shook his head and she lifted his hand to her mouth, kissed his knuckles. "It's not your fault."

He leaned forward and caressed her cheek. She wanted to turn into the caress, wanted to stay like this forever. Her heart was so full of everything she was beginning to feel for this man. Surely he could see it in her eyes. She thought she should pull away, should guard herself better.

But she couldn't.

"I know that. Now." He squeezed her hand and then picked up his fork again. "It took a long time, but I know I wasn't to blame for William's rages. I escaped the brunt of them most of the time. The others…"

Her heart felt as if someone had wrapped it in chains. She was bound to him tighter and tighter with every word.

He shrugged, yet she knew he didn't feel at all carefree about what he said. "I could tell. I knew when he was going to explode. He rarely took it out on me because I didn't push his buttons. I never could understand why the others couldn't see it. I tried to warn them. It never worked. And then Annabelle…"

Cara shuddered at the thought that Annabelle's scars had been caused by her own father. The woman she'd met had been so lovely, so cool and collected. So reserved, hiding behind her hair and her camera. What must she feel every day of her life if her brother felt so much pain simply at the thought of it?

"He beat her because she was beautiful, because she'd dared to want to grow up. She got dressed up and snuck out to a party. When William saw her in her heels and lipstick, he went berserk." He took a deep breath. "I wasn't there. It was all over by the time I'd arrived. Nathaniel and Sebastian tried to stop him, but they were too young, too small. Jacob arrived and hit him."

It was so telling to her that he called his father by his first name. She'd been confused for just a moment, but then she'd understood. William. Not Dad. Not Daddy. Not Father.

She turned the words over in her head. *Daddy.* That was the word that stood out. It still made her ache just to think it. It was a kid's word, but she'd barely been more than a kid when her father had left.

"I don't think it's wrong to feel the way you do, Jack. But he's dead—" she couldn't say *father* when he wouldn't "—and the how no longer matters."

"I feel like I should have done something more for the others. If I'd been the one to kill him, then Jacob wouldn't have…"

"Wouldn't have what?" she asked when he didn't continue.

He shook his head, more to himself than to her. "He wouldn't have left," he said. "Now eat before it gets cold."

She wanted him to keep talking. He was on the edge of something she wanted to hear, but he said nothing more. And she wouldn't push him any further tonight. He'd already said so much, far more than she'd have expected.

When they finished eating, she cleaned the dishes while he made espresso. They drank it at the table on the balcony, along with an aperitif, and then went to bed and fell asleep in each other's arms. It was domestic and peaceful—but Cara didn't fool herself. This was the calm before the storm. And when the storm came, the pain would follow. It always did.

Jack slept fitfully. Beside him, Cara was warm and soft and soundly asleep. But he kept running over the past. He hadn't thought this deeply about it in years, and now he couldn't stop. He kept seeing Jacob's face in the bar. What could Jacob possibly want to say after all these years? Did he expect to just waltz back into everyone's lives and be forgiven for abandoning them?

The others might not have a problem with that, but Jack did. If Jacob had run away once before, what was to stop him from doing so again? Jack wasn't willing to take that chance. Wasn't willing to care again, when caring would lead to disappointment.

Cara snuggled closer to him in her sleep. She was so sensual, so amazing, and he wanted her with a passion he hadn't felt in a long time. He'd wanted women before, but he couldn't remember ever feeling quite this level of desire. There was something strong and elemental between them, something that made sex a necessity rather than just a logical conclusion to their attraction. But he knew better than to allow it to mean more than it did. It was just sex. Hot, passionate, no-holds-barred sex.

As if thinking the words conjured the deed, Cara's hand slipped over his body with a deliberation that said she was no longer asleep. Though he wanted to roll her beneath him and thrust into her body, he waited to see what she would do. She caressed his chest, his abdomen, his hip, his bare buttock, her lips pressing to the hollow of his throat as she nuzzled against him. Though he'd had her only a few hours ago, he was hard and ready for her again.

Without a word, she pushed him onto his back and straddled him, taking him deep within her. She rode him slowly, deliberately, until he couldn't take it anymore. Until he gripped her hips and drove up inside her again and again until she cried out with the force of her release. Her body gripped him, milked him with tiny shudders, and he let go with a harsh cry.

They stayed entwined for the longest time. Jack started to doze, but then she broke the quiet stillness of the night when she said, "I want to tell you something."

Jack yawned. "I'm listening."

She pushed away from him and sat up. The air wafting over his body cooled him and he wanted her against him again. But he resisted reaching for her because it was clear she needed to do this her way.

He could see her outline in the dark, and though he couldn't see the features of her body, he imagined them. The high, pert nipples. Her narrow waist tapered down to flared hips, and the place between her legs—that wonderful place he adored—would still be sensitive to the touch. If he were to slide his fingers into that wetness, she would shudder and moan...

"Jack."

"Yes, darling?"

"You aren't listening."

"What makes you think so?"

"Because your hand is on my breast."

He would have laughed if he didn't sense she

was being serious, so he pulled his hand away
with a sigh. "Sorry. Continue."

"I've been thinking about what you said. About
your, um, father and Jacob—"

"Cara—"

She put a hand over his mouth. "No, listen.
Please."

Her hand fell away and he didn't say a word.

"I can't pretend to know what you've been
through, Jack. And I don't want to make it sound
like I'm trying to compare my experience to yours.
But I want to tell you the truth about my family."

He'd begun to think she wasn't going to tell him
anything. Each time he'd asked, she'd deflected
the conversation without telling him anything
substantial—other than the hurricane and the
deadbeat boyfriend. Perhaps she was embarrassed
that she came from humble roots, or perhaps there
were even darker things in her past than in his.
Whatever the reason, he'd decided she intended
to remain silent about it.

She pulled in a deep breath as if she were gathering her courage, let it out in a rush. "I told you
that my mama lost her house when Katrina hit.
But I didn't tell you that my dad left us shortly
after. I thought they had the perfect marriage, but
it turns out that my father had another family we
didn't know about. He'd been having an affair for
years with a woman in another town. They had a

daughter together." She laughed, the sound breaking off. "I have a sister I didn't find out about until six years ago. I've never even met her."

"Do you want to?" he asked.

She seemed surprised if the way she hesitated were any indication. "I don't know. It's not her fault, and yet..." She twisted the sheets in her hands. He waited for her to get to it in her own time. "I have another sister...Evie. And a little brother. Remy. He's the sweetest thing alive, but he's, um..."

She let out a harsh breath, full of anger and tears he sensed she hadn't let fall yet. "Remy was starved of oxygen at birth and he suffered mental difficulties because of it. He's eighteen now, but he has the mental capacity of a six-year-old."

He reached for her hand, squeezed it. She didn't pull away. "This is why you work so hard," he said, his heart pinching for her. It made so much sense now. Why she was so focused, so independent. Why she'd been so worried about money and why she'd taken a job with Bobby Gold.

She nodded. "Yes. Remy's therapy is subsidized by the state, but only to a point. He needs specialized care. And he's very sensitive to changes. The loss of the house devastated him because he couldn't understand why everything was different. We worked hard to get it back to normal as quickly as we could. Of course, by the time we'd done so, he was used to the trailer we'd been living in."

He knew what came next, what she hadn't yet said. "It must have been difficult for him when your father left."

"Oh, God, you have no idea." She rubbed a hand across her brow. "I haven't spoken to my father in six years, Jack. And watching you with your brother, it began to bother me. What if he wanted to talk to me? What would I do? Would I push him away? Or would I listen? I'm furious with him, and yet I wonder what he might say if I gave him the chance. Not that he wants to say anything," she added. "But if he did..."

He knew what she was trying to say. And he was caught between sympathy for her and the pain of old wounds.

"You think I should have let Jacob speak," he said. Anger roiled beneath the surface, but it was the old anger, not anything new. He wasn't angry with her, didn't feel the need to lash out and defend his actions.

"I can't tell you what to do, Jack. But maybe if you talked to him, you'd know whether it was right to go on being angry or whether it was time to let it go. Maybe you could move forward."

"It was a long time ago. What makes you think I haven't moved on?" Jack demanded. "I don't spend my days thinking about this."

"No, I know you don't. But just like what happened with my family still bothers me, I think you're still stuck with what happened to yours. If you weren't, you wouldn't have gotten so angry."

Jack blew out a harsh breath. He'd gone entire months—years even—without thinking much about the past. Until Jacob returned. Now, he had to think about it—and he didn't like it one bit.

"I'm not sure I can do it, Cara. Jacob was all we had. He was our father figure, much more so than William ever was. And when he was gone, it left a gaping hole in our lives. Lucas tried to fill it, but he failed, as well. I *couldn't* fail. I had no choice."

"It wasn't fair that you had to step into Jacob's and Lucas's shoes," she said. "It must have been hard for you. But you did it. You succeeded where your brothers didn't. But what if Jacob needs you now the way you once needed him?"

He hadn't thought of that. But then he also didn't care. Let Jacob need him—need all of them—if that's what it was. Let him fool the rest of them with his remorse and his return to Wolfe Manor. He couldn't fool Jack.

"Sometimes the past belongs in the past," he said roughly. "Sometimes it's better that way."

She lay down again with a sigh and put her head on his shoulder. She smelled warm and sweet and sensual. Like flowers and sex.

"You're probably right," she said. "I just wanted to say it."

He ran his fingers up her arm. Her skin was so soft, like silk. He liked being here with her like this. The night was dark, conducive to secrets, and he found himself wanting to explain why he felt the way he did.

"I was seventeen when I had to be the head of the household. I had to figure out how to make sure we were okay, how to balance the books and keep everything running smoothly. I also had to deal with the emotional fallout of the younger ones."

"It's a lot of responsibility," she murmured.

"I didn't get to do what I wanted, Cara. Everything I did was for them. When I left school, I took a job in London and commuted from our home in Oxfordshire. I never even went to university. I worked. I didn't play, I didn't party, and I didn't do anything typical for my age."

Her hand curled into a fist on his chest. "You think he robbed you of that."

"Yes." And yet it was more than that. He'd admired Jacob, had wanted to be like him—but when he'd realized that Jacob wasn't as strong as he'd always believed, a part of Jack had feared that he would fail, as well. If Jacob couldn't do it, how could he?

But he had. He'd succeeded where Jacob and

Lucas had failed. The cost had been enormous, however. In some ways, he was still paying it.

"Maybe you need to tell him how you feel," Cara said. "Tell him why you're so angry."

As if that would do any good. If Jacob had cared—if Lucas had cared—they wouldn't have stuck Jack with the responsibility in the first place. They knew why he was angry. They knew why he couldn't forgive and forget.

"Did you ever do that?" he asked. "Did you ever tell your father how you feel about what he did?"

He could feel her head moving as she shook it. "No. But I've never had the chance. You do, Jack."

He sighed. "It won't change what happened. Will you get those years back that you worked so hard to help your mother rebuild her house? Will you get back the dreams you gave up when your father abandoned your family?"

"No," she said softly. And then he felt something hot and wet hit his skin.

He reached for her, pulled her into the cradle of his arms. "I'm sorry, Cara. I'm sorry," he murmured, kissing away her tears.

And then he made her forget everything but him.

CHAPTER TWELVE

FOR the next two weeks Cara shoved aside her doubts and fears about the future. She decided to live each day to the fullest. She didn't ask about her passport and Jack didn't offer. She'd managed to get her bank card canceled and a new one issued and mailed to her at the London address, so she would soon have access to her own money. That was a relief, at least.

Since that night when they'd spoken of their families and their pain, they'd not talked about it again. But in every other way, they'd grown closer. Jack took her to the opera, the theater, to dinner and for long drives in the country. He cooked her breakfast, surprised her with flowers and made love to her so thoroughly that she marveled she'd ever lived without him.

He knew what turned her on, knew how to drive her insane and knew what made her scream with pleasure. This need she had for him was an obsession. All he had to do was look at her—and she

slipped her clothes from her body and shameless-
ly seduced him. They made love in the bathtub,
against the wall, on the floor, in the car, on his
desk and, on one memorable occasion, on the balcony in the middle of the night with all of London
spread out below.

She was utterly shameless when it came to
loving Jack. Because, yes, she'd finally had to
admit to herself that she'd taken the plunge—that
she'd fallen head over heels for Jack Wolfe. She
should have left that first day, but she'd stayed.
And now it was too late, because her heart was
irrevocably lost.

She hadn't told him how she felt because she
had the feeling they were living in a magic bubble—and if she spoke the words, the bubble would
burst and reality would crash down on her once
more.

He made love to her like he couldn't live without her, and yet he'd never spoken a word of tender
feelings for her. He'd praised her body, praised her
skill in bed and in the kitchen when she'd made
him a pot of Mama's gumbo, told her she was
beautiful and sexy and exciting—but he'd never
said a thing that made her think his heart was
engaged.

For Jack, it was all about the physical. Sometimes
they spent the entire day in bed, reading, talking
and laughing between bouts of lovemaking. On

lays like that, they never dressed. They slept and ate and lost themselves in each other.

It was glorious and blissful, but it wasn't enough. She wanted *more*. She wanted to know she wasn't alone in this emotional need for him. She wanted his heart. If she knew she had his heart, then everything would be okay.

Keep telling yourself that, Cara.

"We've been invited to a cocktail party."

Cara turned at the sound of his voice. Her heart squeezed, like it always did, whenever he entered a room. Or, in this case, the balcony. The bruising under his eye was almost completely gone now. He was without doubt the most incredibly handsome male she'd ever seen—with or without a black eye.

"That sounds nice," she replied, smiling as best she could with her thoughts in turmoil. She searched his face for some hint of feeling, but he was carefully controlled as always.

Would she never break through his barriers? Was it a waste of time to try?

"Rupert is an old business partner of mine," he said, picking up her glass and taking a drink of iced water. "We don't need to stay long."

"Fine," she replied. She'd lost the ability to form sentences as she wrestled with her thoughts.

He set the glass down. "Is something wrong, Cara?"

She shrugged, smiled. "Of course not."

He frowned. "We don't have to go at all, if you don't want."

She sighed, wrapped her arms around herself in a protective gesture. "I don't mind going, Jack."

He looked at her a moment more, then came over and kissed her. "Good. I'll let him know we're coming. I have a few more things to take care of and then I'm yours for the rest of the evening."

If only he really was hers, she thought, when he went back inside. But he wasn't. And she didn't really think he ever would be.

The people in Rupert Blasdell's town house glittered. They literally glittered. Cara had never seen so many jewels in her life—and she'd seen some pretty gorgeous ones on women in the casino. Her own neck was bare. In her ears, she wore the same small silver hoops she'd been wearing when she'd first met Jack. She'd splurged on a silver bangle watch a few weeks back and she'd put that on as well. It hadn't been expensive, and she felt the lack of its pedigree keenly tonight.

Which wasn't like her at all, really. She'd never cared about designer names before.

Still, she'd thought she looked pretty good in her pale pink silk sheath, sky-high designer shoes and silver jewelry. Until she'd arrived on the steps of this Mayfair home and seen the jewels pouring from the limos, Bentleys and Rolls Royces.

Jack seemed oblivious. She'd gone inside on his arm, holding her head high, but they'd ended up separated after he'd gotten her another glass of champagne. Now she stood in the middle of a packed room and sipped her champagne more out of nervousness than because she was thirsty.

He'd said it was a cocktail party, not a gala event for the richest people in all of London. She wouldn't be surprised if the queen showed up next. Yes, she and Jack had attended a few events together over the past week, but nothing had been this, well, *fancy*. Even the opera, to which he'd worn a tuxedo and she'd donned a long gown, had seemed like a down-home crawfish boil compared to this.

The crowd parted and she caught sight of Jack talking to a man and a woman. She thought they were a couple until the woman put her hand on Jack's arm. Her fingers caressed him possessively, sliding down his forearm. He pressed the back of her hand to his mouth as she leaned in and said something Cara imagined only he could hear. The man didn't bat an eyelash at her behavior, so clearly they weren't together.

Cara squashed the jealousy that flared to life inside her. Jack was with *her*. Not only that, but there were physical limits to what a man could do.

Even a man as sensual as Jack. And she was confident she kept him far too busy in bed for him to consider straying elsewhere.

For now.

And that was the rub, wasn't it? He wanted her *now*. He was with her *now*. No idea what tomorrow would bring. No idea how much longer it would last. His heart wasn't engaged.

But hers was. Irrevocably. Painfully.

This was why she'd always been independent, why she'd been determined not to need a man. This aching in her soul was the reason why. She felt so stupid, as naive as he'd once called her. She'd wanted to believe in happy ever after, but she hadn't wanted to risk her heart for it. How could she have been so blind? Love was all about heartbreak, whether you wanted it to be or not.

It wasn't containable or controllable. You couldn't orchestrate happiness.

She started to move toward him, but then she was cut off by a couple walking into her path. She stepped back, found herself near the champagne fountain. She started to move away again, but she heard Jack's name and stopped.

Two women stood together on the other side of the fountain, sipping champagne and looking in Jack's direction.

"Look at Sherry trying to get his attention again," one woman said. Long pink fingernails wrapped around the slender flute she held. She was tanned, but Cara didn't imagine it came from a salon. No, this woman had probably gotten that golden color in Saint-Tropez. On a yacht, of course.

"It won't do any good," the other replied. "He has a new mistress."

The woman with the pink nails gaped at her companion. "You don't mean that woman he came with tonight, do you? She cannot possibly be Jack Wolfe's new mistress. She has no polish, no glamour! She's as tall as a stick and not half as appealing!"

"Bob and I saw them at the opera. And I have it on good authority she's staying in his apartment. She's been there since his brother's wedding. American." The woman sniffed.

"I simply cannot believe Jack has gone slumming!"

Cara stiffened. She wanted to hear what else they had to say, but they moved away, heads bent together. Then they burst out laughing. Cara felt the heat of a blush—or was it anger?—prickling her skin beneath her dress. She didn't belong here. She had a sudden urge to go outside, into the night air, and feel the coolness on her skin.

She moved in the opposite direction of the two women, seeking an exit. Surely there was a patio or a veranda—or whatever in the hell they called it around here. She felt like everyone was staring at her. People moved out of her way, cast glances at her, talked behind their hands or their glasses or whispered in each other's ears.

Talking about *her*. About Jack Wolfe's *mistress*.

She was no prude. She didn't care if the whole world knew she was having sex with Jack. But that word—*mistress*—made it sound as if she were paid to have sex with him. It dehumanized her, took away her power in the relationship.

No, the word took away the *relationship*. She and Jack were no longer equals, adults who had a consenting sexual relationship built on attraction and mutual respect for each other. It took away the love she felt for him, cheapened her feelings.

She hated the word, hated the way it made her feel.

"Cara."

She vaguely heard her name, but she didn't stop.

"Cara!" This time, a hand closed around her arm and brought her up short.

Jack. His brows were drawn low over his eyes as he studied her. "Where were you going?"

She couldn't take it any longer. Couldn't stand the idea that he was everything to her and she was nothing but a warm body to him.

"Where's Sherry?"

His expression grew thunderous. "Where did you hear that name?"

She tossed her hair over her shoulder. Jack took a step closer, crowded her toward a screen set near an archway. Her pulse leaped as his fingers slid up her bare arm.

"The same place I heard someone say I was your new mistress," she flung at him.

She didn't know how he managed it, but they were soon outside, in a garden, moving away from the brightly lit house and into the darkness. Voices carried on the night air, people laughing and talking and clinking glasses.

Jack steered her between tall boxwoods, along a path, until they came to a row of stone columns. Cara jerked away and turned, leaning against the stone, thankful for the cold against her heated skin.

Jack gave her no quarter. He pressed his body against hers, trapping her between the stone and him. He gripped her hands, threaded his fingers with hers and raised them above her head.

Her breasts strained against the strapless sheath, her nipples aching with the need to be touched.

No.

"What's gotten into you?" he asked. "Sherry is someone I dated briefly, nothing more. It's you I need, Cara."

His lips dipped to the hollow of her throat,

skimming her heated skin. She tilted her head back, swallowed her pain and anger. Desire blossomed. Always, always the desire.

"I won't be your mistress, Jack."

He leaned back to look down into her face. His silver eyes glittered in the ambient light. The scent of roses surrounded them, cloying and sweet.

"You already are," he said softly.

Pain stabbed into her, made her ache with the hot rush of it. "No," she whispered, her eyes filling with tears. She would not let them fall. It was ridiculous—*this* was ridiculous. Semantics, she told herself. It's only semantics.

But it wasn't. Not to her.

"I'm not a *mistress*, Jack."

His lips nuzzled her skin again, trailed kisses along her jaw, nibbled her earlobe. "Not a mistress, then. Definitely not a mistress."

Then his hot mouth was on hers, and she was opening beneath him, kissing him with all the passion and hunger he always brought to life inside her.

And yet it felt different this time. Sadder, somehow. As if she'd been stripped of something vital to her understanding of what was between them. Because, as he kissed her in the garden of someone else's home, with those fancy people inside that she knew looked down on her, she couldn't summon up the idea that she belonged here with him.

That she belonged with him at all.

Jack let go of her hands, and she couldn't stop herself from twining them around his neck. Her body arched against him as he splayed a hand over her buttock while the other cupped her breast. He flexed his hips and she felt his hardness pressing into her. Her inner core liquefied with need.

Her body wanted him, her heart wanted him and her head wanted him. But her head insisted she had to make a stand, no matter the consequences.

Jack's hand spanned her thigh, lifted her leg to wrap it around him as his fingers slid beneath her hem.

"I want to make you come," he said.

"Jack, I—"

Then he was beneath the lace of her panties, his long fingers finding the sweet center of her pleasure. Cara gasped as sensation rocked through her. She gripped his shoulders, her back arching against the column, her body greedy for the pleasure he could give her.

"You're so beautiful," he said. "I love watching you like this. Come for me, Cara."

She wanted to tell him to stop, but she was incapable of speech. Incapable of pushing him away when she loved him so much. She felt as if she wasn't in control of her own body, as if Jack owned it instead of her.

He slid a finger inside her, and then another. She was close, so close, her body tightening in upon itself almost painfully.

And then she shattered like a thousand stars splintering apart in the heavens. Jack caught her cries with his mouth, drank them greedily while she clung to him, shuddering from the power of her release. In that single moment when she was still suspended between bliss and reality, she prayed it would never end. That she would never have to acknowledge the truth.

But the moment didn't last, of course. Reality came back to her in degrees. The perfume of the roses, the chirping of crickets, the sound of a car somewhere. Then there was the laughter and the sounds of forks hitting delicate china plates that drifted from the house. Closer still, a woman laughed at something a man said.

As the reality of the night set in, Cara shoved against the broad shoulders of the man she loved. He took away her reason, her sense. He made her want him, no matter the consequences to her soul.

He stepped back, his expression wary.

And she suddenly knew that he'd done this in an effort to prove his mastery over her. He hadn't wanted to pleasure her because he loved her, because he couldn't get enough of her. He'd wanted to divert her from any conversation about them, divert her from asking hard questions or wanting something he wasn't ready—or willing—to give.

Fury and hurt roared through her. He'd made her into exactly what she'd sworn she was not—a woman who clung to a man who didn't love her because she couldn't face the alternative; because a life with him was preferable to a life without him, no matter how constrained that life may be.

Mistress.

This had not been about equality; it had been about dominance. And she despised him for it.

Cara straightened her dress. She had no idea what her hair and makeup were like now. No doubt she looked like a woman who'd been having sex in the garden during a house party. Shame filled her to the brim, threatened to bubble over and turn into angry tears.

"I want to leave now," she said.

"We've only just arrived," he replied. As if it made a difference. As if she cared. "It would be rude to leave so soon."

Cara thrust her chin in the air. "You don't find it rude to leave the party for a tryst in the garden, but it's rude to go home?" She shook her head angrily. "I'm going, Jack. With or without you."

He took another step away, ran a hand through his hair. "Yes, of course. We'll go." And then, because he had to be as sensitive to the currents whipping between them as she was, "I'm sorry, Cara."

"Sorry for what?" she shot back. "For making me into your mistress or for making me care for you? Or sorry for what just happened?"

He was so remote, so untouchable. "I'm sorry for hurting you. You deserve more than this."

"I know I do," she said, her voice barely more than a whisper. The tears of rage and frustration she'd been holding back spilled over. She did deserve more, damn him! She deserved everything he had to give.

But he was too caught up in the past to let himself go. Jack Wolfe refused to let anyone inside. She'd known it and she'd stayed with him, anyway. Her fault for being so damn naive.

As much as it hurt her to realize it, she had to leave him now, before he took what was left of her soul and crushed it to powder.

"You *are* capable of more, Jack," she said. "But apparently I'm not the one who can make you see it."

CHAPTER THIRTEEN

THEY took a limo back to his apartment. The ride passed in silence, Cara sitting as far away from him as she could get. If he touched her, she feared her resolve would crumble. In spite of everything, her body still hummed with need. All she required was his touch to set spark to the tinder and she would go up in flame.

When they exited the elevator into his apartment, she found the courage to speak. Though they were alone in this space where she'd been so happy with him, there was room to maneuver. She didn't have to be so near him, didn't have to smell his scent and listen to his breathing. She could stop the need to turn her face into his chest and just ask him to hold her if she could put distance between them.

"Am I ever going to be anything more than a *mistress* to you?" she asked, the words biting as she said them.

He turned to her, hands in pockets. He seemed

so remote, so cool. "Still looking for the happy ever after, Cara?"

She trembled with helpless fury. And sadness. Such overwhelming sadness. "I believe it's possible to be happy with one person, yes. I believe it's possible to love and be loved and never need or want anyone else."

His eyes were flat. So flat and empty. "It's a little girl's fantasy," he said, his voice hard. "You should know this as well as I do. Look at our parents, sweetheart. I don't know about yours, but mine defined the word *dysfunctional*. And my father kept on doing it even after my mother was dead."

"Just because our parents didn't get it right doesn't mean we have no chance."

His bark of laughter was not reassuring. "You're so naive, Cara." He closed the distance between them and grabbed her arms. "Why do you have to want more from me? Why can't you just be happy with what we have *right now?*"

Tears pressed against the backs of her eyes. "What do we have, Jack? Tell me what we have, because I want to know."

His face twisted, but whether from rage or frustration she did not know. And then he crushed his mouth down on hers. It was a hard kiss, a kiss of domination, of fear, of desperation.

Though she didn't mean to do it, she kissed him

back. Cara infused all her hope and heartbreak into that single kiss. Anyone witnessing their kiss would know they were engaged in a battle.

There was nothing tender in this kiss. It was all-out war, a fight for domination on the field of battle.

Somehow, Cara found the strength to break away first. She was breathing hard, her emotions whipping her with bitterness as she put a steadying hand on the back of a couch.

Jack stumbled backward a step and ripped his tie loose. His chest rose and fell as rapidly as hers. It gratified her to know he wasn't unaffected, and yet despair hovered behind the pain she felt.

Would he really let it end this way? Was he so determined not to let anyone in that he would throw away a chance at happiness?

Or maybe, Cara thought, he was right. Maybe he *was* giving all he was capable of giving. Maybe she was being unfair in asking for more. Why couldn't she be happy with what they had now? Why did she want more?

Because I deserve it.

Leaving Jack was the right thing to do. She knew it in her heart, no matter how her heart seemed to be splitting in two at the thought. How could she ever rely on him if she didn't trust that he felt the way she did? Would she turn out like Mama, loving a man who deceived her and left her brokenhearted, if she were to settle for anything less than the love she deserved?

"I care about you," he said, breaking into her tormented thoughts. "I want you."

Cara sucked in a shaky breath. "I'm sorry, Jack, but that's not good enough for me. Because I do want the fantasy. I want love and marriage, even though it terrifies me, and I want to be someone's life and soul. I want to be with a man who can't live without me just as I can't live without him."

His laugh was bitter. "You just said love terrifies you. Because you *know* it doesn't last, Cara. You have your parents' example, just as I have mine. People *leave* when you need them most."

She shook her head. A tear slipped down her cheek. "I can't be like you, Jack. As much as it scares me to ever rely on another human being, I want that chance. I want to try, at least. I want to share my life with the man I love, and I want him to share his with me."

His eyes were so full of pain and frustration. She wanted to go to him, wanted to wrap her arms around him and tell him everything would be all right. But she wasn't really sure if it would ever be all right. She watched him, waiting for his response. Waiting for him to acknowledge what she'd just told him.

But if he understood that she'd confessed her love for him, he didn't show it.

"What do you want from me?"

"I think you know."

"This has been good between us, Cara. It doesn't need to end."

She pulled in a deep breath. "It has been good, you're right. But it's not enough. I want more. I don't want to go to parties and have people whisper behind my back that I'm just another mistress. I want people to know we're together, that I've chosen you every bit as much as you've chosen me. I don't want to be just another bought and paid-for companion."

And she was, wasn't she? Ever since she'd accepted his offer to come to London for the wedding, the balance of power had been thrown off. As much as she'd tried to convince herself it was a legitimate job, the truth was far different. Because she'd been fated to fall into bed with him from the moment he'd arrived at her table in Nice.

"You can't listen to gossip, Cara. People will try to hurt you if you let them."

"They wouldn't try if they didn't think it was true."

His jaw was hard, his eyes glittering. He swore vehemently.

"Fine, we'll get married if that's what it takes to make you happy."

Cara's heart skipped a beat. She couldn't imagine what it had cost him to say that. She would have laughed if her heart weren't breaking.

"Oh, Jack. You just don't get it, do you? It's not about marriage." She walked over to him, placed a hand on his chest. Felt the thundering pulse of his heart. "It's about what's in here. I want to know *you*. I want you to let me inside. And I'm not sure you ever will."

He gripped her hand where it lay against his heart. He looked so serious and so tortured at once.

"You do know me. As well as anyone."

She shook her head sadly. "But for how long, Jack?"

"As long as it lasts," he said.

"I can't do it. I'm sorry. I should have gone sooner, but—"

"What?" he prompted when she didn't continue.

Cara shrugged. "I didn't want to. I fell for you, Jack. And I kept hoping you'd love me, too."

"I care for you." His voice sounded as if it had been scraped over sandpaper.

Poor Jack. It was such a hard admission for him. And it was all she'd ever get.

She took a step back, wrapped her arms around her body. "It's time I went home. I need to find another job, need to move forward with my life.…"

He swore. "Go, then," he bit out.

Her eyes filled with tears. "I still need my passport—"

"It's here."

Cara blinked. "You have it? Since when? Why didn't you tell me?"

"It came two days ago."

Two days? He'd had her passport for two days and he'd not told her about it? Was this why? Had he wanted to avoid exactly the conversation they were having now?

"Why didn't you tell me?" she repeated.

He walked over to the kitchen island, retrieved an envelope and tossed it onto the bar near her. "Does it matter? You have it now."

Cara picked up the envelope and opened it. Her bank card was inside, as well.

"Your clothes and other belongings will arrive soon."

"You managed to get everything from Bobby?" She'd hoped she'd get her passport back, but she'd never expected she would see anything else she'd taken to Nice with her. Fortunately, it had only been two suitcases full. Nothing that wasn't replaceable.

Jack laughed, but there was no humor in it. "Believe it or not, Cara, I'm quite frightening when I'm not bound and beaten. Bobby was only too happy to cooperate once the situation was explained to him."

Cara shivered at the menace in his voice. Having spent the past couple of weeks with him, she could fully believe he would intimidate Bobby under the right circumstances. He was immensely wealthy and extremely powerful. All of which she'd shoved to the back of her mind while she'd been here. She'd cared about him as a person, and though she'd known how wealthy he was, she'd been able to forget it when it was just the two of them together.

A mistake, clearly. If she'd remembered, if she'd forced herself to remember, she'd have known this could never work out between them. She had nothing he needed—not even love.

God, could her heart hurt any worse that it did right this moment? Could she feel any more hopeless?

"Thank you," she said. It was the only thing she was capable of. Her throat hurt with all she wanted to say. She wouldn't let it happen, though. It was too late. Useless. He didn't love her and he never would. He'd only wanted to control her, just as he controlled everything around him. It was his shield, she realized, his attempt at making sure no one could hurt him ever again.

He stood with his hands in his pockets once more. He looked…angry, helpless, frustrated. All the things she felt, as well.

"You don't have to go," he said.

Cara pulled in a deep breath. It was so tempting to stay, anyway, to cast aside her fears and doubts and go to him. They would be explosive in bed, as always, and she could forget that he didn't love her when they were lost in each other.

She closed her eyes. *No.* She couldn't forget. That was the problem. Everything had changed and she couldn't turn back the clock no matter how much she might wish it.

"I'm afraid I do, Jack," she said. "There's nothing left for me here."

CHAPTER FOURTEEN

SHE'D been gone for a week. Jack shoved back from the computer and stared at the sky out the window. Why was the sky blue? It should be steel-gray, the color of sadness and tears and pain, not bright and happy and buoyant.

Unbidden, the memory of their last night together crashed into his mind. He'd been an ass. He'd seen the despair on her face when she'd turned to him in Rupert Blasdell's house—and he'd simply *known*.

Known he was losing her. Known she was about to demand more than he could give her and that the end was fast coming upon them.

He'd been prepared to accept it. He'd expected it, after all. But then, as he'd stood there and looked into her expressive eyes—as he'd seen himself reflected in them, not as he truly *was*, but as she saw him—he'd felt so damn desperate, so torn and aching and he'd wanted her again. He'd wanted to make her forget what she was about to say, forget what she was thinking. He'd wanted to keep seeing himself through her eyes.

Because that Jack was better than he was.

But he'd failed. Instead of making her forget, he'd pushed her farther and faster to the end. He'd taken her love and twisted it against her in an effort to keep her. He'd wanted to dominate her, control her, and he'd acted without thought.

He'd never forget the way she'd looked at him in the garden, when he knew he'd gone too far. She'd been so disillusioned, so angry. He'd done that to her, and he'd hated himself for it in that moment.

Damn her for making him feel so much. Damn her, because he missed her.

Jack stood and went into the kitchen. It was empty, as always. The living room was empty. The balcony. The bedroom.

And suddenly, he didn't want to be alone. He was so damn tired of being alone. Grabbing his keys, he left the apartment and took the elevator down. Then he walked to the pub on the corner and went inside. It was still early, and though the pub was occupied, it wasn't as lively as it would be later.

He wanted the noise, the press of bodies and yes, even the empty companionship of a woman, if he met one who interested him. A few hours in bed with another woman would surely take his mind off Cara.

Except the thought of taking another woman to bed was strangely abhorrent.

Jack found a corner table and sat down. A waitress came over and he ordered a pint. He closed his eyes and leaned back on the booth seat.

Cara.

"Hello, Jack."

His eyes snapped open. Jacob stood in front of the table, an apparition from the past. The old anger and pain roiled in his belly, but he didn't feel the instinctive need to lash out that he had only a couple of weeks ago. He was too drained from thoughts about Cara to work up more than a mild dislike for his brother.

"What the hell are you doing here, Jacob?"

Jacob's dark hair was tousled as always. His black eyes seemed so bleak that Jack almost softened.

Almost, but not quite. If Jacob was tortured by what he'd done, it was nothing less than he deserved.

"I came to talk to you."

Jack snorted. "What'd you do, lurk outside my apartment and follow me here? How the mighty have fallen," he finished sarcastically.

One corner of Jacob's mouth lifted in a mocking grin. "Hardly. I was on my way to your place when I saw you leave. So yes, in that sense I followed you here. Sue me."

He was on the verge of telling Jacob to get the hell out, but then he thought of Cara. *"What do you think your brother wanted? Maybe if you talked to him...you could move forward."*

He *had* moved forward. But his curiosity was piqued for the first time in years. What was Jacob so intent on saying? It wouldn't change anything, but maybe if he listened, he could tell Cara he'd done so.

Tell Cara?

"What do you want?" Jack bit out.

"I want to apologize," Jacob said. "For leaving."

A chill crept over Jack. "It's a bit late, don't you think?"

Jacob's nostrils flared. A sign of annoyance he recognized from their childhood. Jack practically laughed. So Jacob wasn't here to play the penitent, after all. It was a relief, in a way. It made it easier for Jack to shrug off Jacob's reappearance in their lives. He didn't know what Jacob was up to, but he stuck by his belief that his brother wasn't here to stay. The minute it got difficult, Jacob would run. Just like before.

"I'm sorry you feel that way," Jacob said. "I know what it took for you to fill my shoes, and I'm sorry you had to do it."

"Not sorry enough to come back, though."

Jacob took the seat across from him. Jack would

have protested, but his beer arrived. He took a drink and waited for what Jacob would say next. But Jacob looked away, like he was thinking of something, and Jack's temper frayed.

"As touching as this reunion is for me," he said, "I'd really like to be alone. So if you have something to say, say it. If not, get out and let me drink in peace."

Jacob's dark head swung back around. His black eyes glittered with anger. "You've turned into quite a bastard, haven't you, Jack? Is that why the pretty lady left you?"

Everything inside him went dark and still. The urge to reach across the table and plant a fist in Jacob's face was strong.

"Leave her out of this," he growled.

"Why? Is she important to you? Is *anything* important to you, other than your own grief and rage?"

Jack's gut burned. The beer went down hard and he signaled the waitress for another. "You're a fine one to talk about what's important, aren't you, Jacob? You can't do important. You'd rather run away from it."

"My God. You've been shutting people out for so long you just don't know how to do anything differently."

A prickle of awareness slipped across his soul. Cara had accused him of shutting people out. Or shutting *her* out. It was safer that way, wasn't it? If you didn't let anyone in, they couldn't hurt you when they left.

The waitress arrived with his beer. "He's leaving," Jack said when she asked Jacob what he wanted. She shrugged and went away.

And suddenly Jack was tired of being angry. He just wanted this conversation over with. He wanted to drink until Cara was a blurry memory, and he wanted to be alone.

"Look, whatever you're here for, whatever you think you're going to accomplish by renovating Wolfe Manor, I don't care. It's been too many years, and there's too much water under the bridge to go back now."

"You think I'm leaving again," Jacob said.

Jack shrugged. "You know, I really don't want to do this. You don't have to come here and talk to me and apologize and try to fix anything. It's too late for that. As soon as you run across something you don't like, some difficulty, you'll leave again."

"I don't blame you for thinking so, but I'm not leaving, Jack."

"The others may have fallen for your lies, but you're wasting your time with me."

"Yeah, I guess so." Jacob stood. "Maybe we can talk about this some day, but clearly it won't be today. When you're ready, I'll be here."

Jack looked at his brother, really looked at him for the first time in twenty years. There was anger and sorrow and regret in his eyes—and determination. Maybe that determination would see him through. Maybe he'd find the strength to face whatever demons he'd been running from.

But Jack still couldn't accept that Jacob wouldn't pull up stakes when things got tough. He'd spent too many years living in the shadow of Jacob's mistakes, too many years trying to make it right again.

And yet a part of him wanted to believe. A very tiny part that missed the way they used to be close. It surprised him, that feeling. He hadn't looked back in years. He made decisions and moved forward because it was a waste of time to dwell on the might-have-beens.

"We'll see," was all he could say.

Jacob nodded. Whether he took the words as an admission that a conversation was possible or a challenge that he would leave again, Jack didn't know. Or care.

After Jacob had gone, Jack toyed with the cold mug of beer but didn't take another drink. His head was tangled up with Jacob, with Cara, with events of the past. He thought of his brothers and sister, of the hell they'd been through. He thought of Cara, with her wide green eyes and her kissable lips—and he missed her like hell.

She'd filled that empty space inside him. She'd made him laugh. She'd made him think.

But not enough, apparently. Because he'd completely missed what she'd been saying to him about love and living and being. She was right that he never let anyone inside. And he suddenly wished he hadn't pushed her away.

Because he realized, as he sat there, that she wasn't just a woman he'd met in a casino in Nice. She wasn't just a woman he'd taken to a wedding, a woman he'd had incredible sex with.

She was *the* woman. The only woman who'd ever gotten to him on more than a superficial level. She was the one who filled his thoughts when he woke, his thoughts when he went to bed at night and his thoughts every moment in between.

She was the only woman he'd ever considered committing to, the only one he'd ever thought of marrying—even if his offer had been sullen and desperate and merely an attempt to keep her from leaving.

It hit him then that he was just like Jacob. That when he'd encountered something he couldn't handle, he'd run away from it. Emotionally, he was a coward. He'd castigated Jacob for leaving, and yet he'd left, too. He'd left the only woman he'd ever loved because he feared what loving her would mean.

He hadn't left her physically, but he'd pushed

her away. Because he'd been determined not to fall in love with her, not to need her on an emotional level because needing meant vulnerability.

But the joke was on him because he did need her. Hell, he loved her! He'd been able to mask the emotional truth behind the physical, to convince himself that's all it was, but the truth was shining down on him now with the force of a thousand brilliant suns.

He couldn't hide from that kind of illumination. He couldn't escape it, even if he wanted to. Jack shoved up from the booth and tossed a couple of notes on the table. He didn't want to escape the truth. He wasn't running away ever again.

New Orleans was far muggier than London had been. Cara hopped from the streetcar and walked the block to work. She'd only been home two weeks, but she'd managed to get a job in the casino. If Bobby had been planning to blacklist her, he must not have gotten around to it yet. She'd fully expected, when she'd applied, that she would never get a call back.

Instead, the manager had called her a few days later and asked when she could start. Tonight was her fifth night, and though it wasn't as exciting as Nice had been, she was happy enough. She was through with adventures for the time being.

Mama, Evie and Remy were fine, and the money

she'd brought home had done so much good. She hadn't intended to take a dime of Jack's money after what had happened between them, but when she'd gotten home and seen Remy's sweet face, she'd known it was the right thing to do.

She hadn't even had to ask Jack for it. While she'd been on her way home, he'd deposited over seventy thousand dollars into her account. It was far more than their agreement, and even though the money was welcome, she'd already withdrawn the overpayment plus two thousand dollars for her clothing, and sent it back to him.

She would take what he owed her, for her family's future, but she wouldn't accept a penny more.

Cara paused to look at the palm trees lining the street. They made her think of Nice, and thinking of Nice made her remember that first night she'd met Jack. He'd been so vibrant, so much larger than life. He'd made the other men at the table pale in comparison. She'd recognized her attraction to him, but she hadn't recognized the danger he represented to her heart.

That had taken a little longer.

Cara went into the employee area and put her things away. She had to stop thinking about Jack Wolfe. He was out of her life, and it was better that way.

She stopped in the ladies' bathroom to check

her makeup and hair before going onto the floor. The eyes looking back at her in the mirror were so forlorn.

"Stop it," she said to her reflection. "He's gone. He didn't love you and the sooner you stop loving him, the better."

"Amen, girlfriend."

Cara turned as Jeannie LaSalle emerged from one of the stalls.

"I didn't know anyone was here," Cara said.

Jeannie shrugged. "Sorry. But I had to reply." She washed her hands and dug out her lipstick from her purse. "You can't let a man ruin your day, honey. There's always another one around the corner. What you gotta do once you get thrown from the horse is get right back on again."

"I don't think I'm ready for that."

Jeannie pursed her red lips as she patted her bleached blond hair. "The first time is the hardest. You just gotta do it. Trust me, you'll feel much better."

Cara didn't really think so, but once she was at her table, dealing to the players, she got mad that Jack was occupying so many of her thoughts. Did he think of her so frequently?

Cara snorted. He probably didn't think of her at all. He'd probably called Sherry the ex the moment Cara was gone and even now was rollng around in bed with her. Entwined in her arms. Kissing her, thrusting into her body—

Stop.

"So what are you doing after you get off work onight?"

Cara jerked her attention to the man sitting o her right. He was holding his cards lazily, his mouth cocked in a confident grin, his blue eyes ntense as they stared at her. She swallowed.

"Going home," she said.

He shrugged. "Maybe we could get a drink."

"I don't—" She cleared her throat. Get back on he horse, right? *Oh, God.* "Maybe."

His grin turned megawatt. He wasn't unattract-ve. In fact, he was downright cute with his tousled sandy-blond hair, high cheekbones and blindingly white teeth.

But her heart ached at the thought of spending ime with any man who wasn't Jack.

Damn him. He was *not* going to control her life now that he was no longer in it.

"Are you from around here?" she asked, forc-ng herself to smile as she did so.

"Texas," he said. "You?"

"Born and raised." She dealt another hand.

"Name's Rand," he said, leaning to the side to check her out. He grinned at her again.

"Cara," she forced out, her heart pounding a million miles an hour. She could do this, she really could. It was just banter. A drink, maybe. Nothing else. Talking to this man didn't mean she was going home with him.

"I've about decided that Louisiana girls are the prettiest," Rand said.

"Aren't you sweet," she managed to say without rolling her eyes.

The hand ended and Cara collected the cards.

"Maybe we can turn that drink into dinner," Rand said.

"Maybe."

"She's not going to dinner with you," a voice growled.

Cara's head snapped up. She blinked at the man standing on the other side of the table. He was tall, menacing—and so damn handsome he broke her heart.

Rand was looking at Jack like he'd just taken away a lollipop. "I think she can decide for herself," Rand said. "Isn't that right, Cara?"

Oh, God.

She swallowed. Jack arched an eyebrow as he stared at her, his silver eyes glittering with heat and anger.

A rush of hot emotion flooded her, followed by a quickening current of doubt. *Why* was he here? Was this some kind of joke?

"I haven't decided what I'm doing later," Cara

said, her eyes never leaving Jack's. "I have no commitments."

She emphasized the word *commitments*.

Jack pulled a chair out and sat down. "Tell you what," he said to Rand, his gaze still not leaving hers, "I'll play you for her."

Cara sputtered. Rand grinned. "All right, dude," he said. "But I hope you don't mind losing."

Cara smacked the cards onto the table. "Gentlemen, your stakes are your casino chips. There are no other bets permitted."

Jack shrugged. "Fine. Whoever has the most chips gets to stay at this table. The loser disappears."

"Sounds fair," Rand agreed.

Fury bubbled in her veins, but she dealt the cards. One hand turned into two. Two turned into four. On the fifth hand, Jack laid down his cards with that infuriating blankness she'd come to expect out of him. Rand had no idea what was about to hit him.

"Four of a kind. The gentleman wins," she pronounced.

Rand whistled. Then he put his hand out and shook Jack's. "No hard feelings, buddy. Good luck."

She watched Rand go, stunned at how easily he accepted the loss. He'd be at another table in moments, flirting with another dealer. And he'd probably get that drink, and dinner, and a whole lot more besides.

She felt like an idiot. And she felt hot and angry and achy all at once. The man across the table from her seemed so calm and all she wanted to do was wrap her hands around his neck and choke him.

And then she wanted to kiss the living daylights out of him.

"What are you doing here?" she asked, tossing the cards out in rapid succession. There were no other players at her table. She wondered if he'd somehow arranged that, too.

Jack picked up the cards. "Gambling."

"I can see that," she said crisply. "Why are you gambling, and why are you doing it in New Orleans?"

He folded the hand and met her even stare. "Because you're here."

Cara fumed. "Wonderful. Now why don't you go away and leave me alone?"

"I can't."

Her heart was never going to survive this. It thundered out of control. Her skin was so hot that she wished she could unbutton her white shirt and fan herself. The only way she was getting back to normal was if he left. "I want you to go, Jack."

"And I want to talk to you."

"You had your chance. What could you possibly want to say now?"

He looked out over the casino. The bells of the slots were ringing, people were talking and laughing, and the air, though cooled by massive air-conditioning units, felt heavy. She waited helplessly, because she couldn't storm away if she wanted to keep her job. He had her trapped, and no doubt he knew it.

His gaze settled on her again. "I have a lot to say. But I don't want to do it here."

A couple walked over and asked if they could join the game. Cara smiled and did her job, though her emotions were in turmoil. Jack stayed at the table for the next hour. When he finally got up and left, she breathed a sigh of relief. She didn't know why he was here. Two weeks ago, he'd let her walk out as if he didn't care that she was leaving. As if he could replace her in his bed as easily as walking into a store and buying a new shirt.

Which, she'd decided, he probably could.

He didn't return for the rest of her shift. By the time she got off work, she was angry with herself for caring. She'd kept expecting him to return. She'd looked for him, watched the entrances for any sign of him and casually walked through the casino on her breaks.

Jack had disappeared.

Which was no doubt for the best.

It was nearly midnight when she emerged onto the palm-lined street, and the air was still heavy with heat and humidity. Cara shouldered her bag to begin the walk to the streetcar stop.

"You are not seriously thinking of walking alone at night, are you?"

She spun around to find Jack watching her. With all the people mingling on the steps of the casino, she hadn't seen him standing there when she'd exited.

"It's not far," she said.

He came over and took her bag off her shoulder. "I'll walk with you."

"It's not necessary, Jack."

"I want to."

"And you always get what you want, don't you?" she said bitterly.

He shook his head. She was tall, but he was so much taller, and he towered over her, his presence both comforting and disturbing. She wanted to wrap her arms around him and she wanted to run away from him all at once. It hurt so much to see him again. And he was oblivious.

"I don't, actually," he said.

They walked several steps away before she spun around to face him. The street was well lit, but they were alone this far from the entrance. The air was so thick. She could smell the Mississippi flowing by, could hear the relentless roll of it in her soul. Nothing stopped the river, not even the levees. When the Mississippi grew furious, it rolled farther and faster than ever, devastating those in its path.

Jack was like that, she thought. He was unstoppable. And he devastated anyone in his path. Anyone who dared to love him.

"What do you want from me, Jack? Why have you come all this way? I want to know right now, because I'm not walking another step and waiting for you to decide when the time is right to speak. Say it now, or don't say it at all."

He laughed, a surprised bark of laughter. It warmed her from within, though she wouldn't let him know it. She had to be cool and collected, had to be prepared for whatever he unleashed.

"Why did you send that money back?"

Cara blinked. Her heart seemed to shrivel in her chest. Because, yes, like a fool, she'd hoped he'd come for more.

"You overpaid me. The deal was for fifty thousand, minus two for the clothes."

"And I paid you fifty thousand."

"No, you paid me nearly eighty." This was inane! Why were they discussing this?

"That's the exchange rate, sweetheart."

Cara's jaw dropped. And then she turned without a word and strode down the street. He'd come all this way to argue about money? Because he'd paid her in pounds sterling—or maybe in euros; hell if she knew—when she'd meant dollars?

It was ridiculous.

He caught her arm and spun her around. Cara tried to jerk away, but he wouldn't let go. Dropping her bag, he pushed her against the wall and trapped her there. Cara's eyes closed. He was so warm, so hard, and she'd missed him so much. His scent wrapped around her. She wanted nothing more than to tilt her head up and beg him to kiss her.

"Let me go," she ground out between clenched teeth.

"I can't," he said.

"Jack, for God's sake—"

"I love you, Cara."

She went completely still. A tremor flowed from his body to hers. But no, she had to be imagining it.

His head dipped and his lips touched hers. The kiss was light, so light and tentative, and her heart blossomed.

Her hands curled into fists on his chest—and then she pushed him away. "Stop, just stop."

He did, but the tremor was still there. Or maybe she was imagining it. Maybe it was the jarring of traffic on the road—not that anything had passed recently—or maybe the river was roiling against its barriers so hard it shook the city.

"I can't do this," she said, as much to herself as to him. Her heart was still so raw. It had only been two weeks since she'd left London—a little over a month since she'd met him—and she didn't know when she would ever feel normal again.

She was certain he cared about her—he'd told her so back in London—and certain he needed her physically as much as she needed him.

But he did not love her. He couldn't. How could he go from that cold, remote, disconnected man he'd been for most of his life to a man capable of letting her inside his heart in only two weeks?

It was impossible, no matter how much she wanted it to be true.

His hands dropped to his sides. She reached out and ran her palm along his cheek. His beautiful cheek.

"I appreciate that you want to try, Jack. But we both know you aren't capable of doing this. And it's okay. It really is."

Blindly, she reached for her bag and slipped around him. She felt…bereft. She wanted to turn back to him, wanted what he'd said to be true, but she knew better. How could she ever trust that he wouldn't wake up one day and realize he'd been wrong? That he'd pushed himself into something he wasn't capable of simply because he enjoyed the sex?

She'd seen the reality of that before, and she wasn't prepared to experience it firsthand.

"I had no idea you were a coward, Cara."

His voice cracked across her ears like a whip. She stumbled to a halt and turned around.

He closed the distance between them, though he did not touch her this time. But he was so close, his presence so overwhelming. She wanted to step back, but she did not.

"You're afraid," he said. "You claim that you love me, that you want more from me, but you don't want to give it yourself, do you? You used this to push me away, just as I pushed you away for loving me."

"You're wrong—"

"But the truth is," he continued over top of her, "that we're both afraid and we did everything possible to make the other one leave."

"That's not true—"

He gripped her shoulders. "It *is,* Cara."

She felt her lip begin to tremble. Because she *was* scared, damn him. What if he really did love her? And what if she gave her heart to him only to have it smashed to bits someday down the road when he'd stopped loving her?

It had been easier to walk away while she still could.

"Listen to me," he said roughly. "I told you I couldn't give you more, but I was wrong. I've been blaming my brothers for leaving the family, for abandoning their duty while I had to stick around and make everything work. And I learned how to do it. I made it work by committing myself to doing it. But I let my ability to trust, my ability to love, atrophy. If I didn't feel, then no one could hurt me."

"Jack..." He shredded her heart and soul with his confession. He'd suffered so much, was still suffering, and she hated it. But she was afraid, too. What if he let himself feel now, but his feelings changed later? How would she survive it?

"I saw Jacob after you left. And I realized that I was just like him. In trying to be what I needed to be for everyone, I became what I despised. I was there in body, but I'd let my spirit run away a long time ago."

A tiny tendril of hope began to unfurl inside her. "You talked to him?"

He shrugged. "I could have done better, perhaps, but we spoke briefly."

"Did it make you feel better at all?"

He blew out a breath. "I didn't think so at the time. But maybe it did. Because it helped me to see what I'd been doing. With you. With my life."

Cara bowed her head. His grip on her shoulders eased. "I want to believe you, Jack. But we're so different. I don't belong in your world—"

He said a very obscene word. "You belong wherever you want to belong, Cara. I've never me anyone like you. You're stronger and more honor able than anyone I know. Who else would refuse to throw a fifteen-million-euro card game when so much was at stake personally?"

"I think a lot of people would. I don't think I'm unique in that."

Jack laughed. "Maybe not unique, but damr rare among the people I know. And I love you for it."

"Now I know you're not serious," she said. "Because if that's why you love me, what happens when you find out there are a whole lot of people who would do what I did? I could introduce you to quite a few while you're here—"

He stopped her with his mouth. She vaguely thought she should push him away again, but she really didn't want to. Just one more kiss. One more night. She could do that, right?

"It's not the only reason I love you," he said against her lips. A shiver trickled down her spine. His tongue traced the seam of her mouth, dipped inside to tangle with hers again.

"Oh, God, Cara," he groaned as she arched against him. "I love you for so many reasons. Reasons that have nothing to do with that gorgeously wicked tongue of yours, though I'm damned if I can think when you've been kissing me like this."

"You kissed me," she protested.

"I'd like to kiss more of you," he said. "Much, much more."

Cara put her hand against his chest and took a step back. She needed space to breathe, space to think. He addled her brain. Liquefied her insides. Made her want to do utterly shameless things with him.

Right here, right now.

"I want to know what you expect to happen now that you've told me you love me."

His smile was confident, sure and completely heart-stopping. "What I expect is that you will agree to marry me. As soon as possible. Tonight would be best, but I'll wait until tomorrow—"

"You can't get married that fast anywhere, Jack."

He put a finger over her lips. "Yes, you can, sweet Cara. Las Vegas. But if that's unacceptable, if you must have a big wedding for your family, then I will wait for that day."

He took his finger away and kissed her, a quick peck that had her stretching up to him even as he pulled away and continued, "And to prove how serious I am, how desperately I want to spend the rest of my life with you, I vow not to make love to you until we are married. Whether that day is tomorrow or six months from now, your chastity is assured."

Joy was beginning to bubble up inside her soul. And certainty: the certainty this was absolutely right, that *he* was right for her and that their love would last forever.

"What if I don't want to be chaste?" she asked, slipping her arms around his neck and arching against him.

His body was stone. Hard, hot stone. He closed his eyes and groaned. Then he opened them and speared her with a glare.

"You will be, like it or not, until the day we are married."

Cara smiled, her heart racing ahead and making her almost dizzy. This was really happening. She was really going to do this. She was going to take the biggest chance of her life—and she wasn't scared any longer.

"Did you bring your plane, Jack Wolfe?"

His answering grin stole her breath. "I did indeed."

"Vegas?" she asked.

"Vegas."

EPILOGUE

THEY were married in Las Vegas before the sun set the next day. And they were making love in a penthouse suite not an hour later. Though it had only been less than two weeks since they'd last been together, this time was like the first time. Jack worshipped her body with his own, bringing her to climax again and again before taking his own pleasure.

Later, when she'd recovered sufficiently, Cara returned the favor, teasing and taunting him to the edge of control before taking him over the peak.

They fell into a deep sleep, and then woke again before sunrise to make love when everything was quiet and still. When it was over, Cara fell asleep again. Her dreams were filled with Jack, and when she woke, he was there with a tray of food and a bouquet of fresh-cut roses.

"Do you think your mother minds very much that she couldn't be here for the wedding?" Jack asked as she smeared jelly on the last slice of toast.

Her heart turned over as she looked at him. He was clad in a pair of silk boxers—and that only so he could answer the door when room service came, she imagined. His hair was tousled, and his easy smile stole her breath away.

"So long as we have the big wedding back home, she doesn't care that we're already married. She couldn't have left Remy, anyway. He wouldn't understand."

"No, I don't suppose he would."

Mama had been so happy for her, and she'd loved Jack on sight. And when they eventually had the church wedding back in New Orleans for friends and family, Mama would be the proudest woman alive.

"What?" Jack said a few moments later, and she knew she'd been staring at him.

"I'm just thinking how much I love you. And how grateful I am for what you're doing for Remy."

The full-time nurse Jack had suggested they hire would make such a difference in Remy's life. In all their lives. Mama wouldn't have to worry so much about her son anymore, and Evie would no longer have to take turns watching Remy. She could pursue her own goals and have the life a twenty-three-year-old should have.

With additional therapy, Remy would be able to cope with changes much better than he did now. It was more than Cara had ever dreamed she would be able to provide.

"Your family is my family now. And your mother's a wonderful woman."

"You're just saying that because she told you to marry me quick before I changed my mind."

He leaned down and kissed her. "You weren't changing your mind."

He went over and opened his briefcase. When he dropped a thick packet on her tray, she frowned. "What's this?"

Jack's smile was very self-satisfied. Like the proverbial cat that ate the canary, she decided. "Open it."

Cara ripped open the packet and pulled out a thick sheaf of papers. Her jaw dropped as she realized what they were. "These are shares in Bobby's Nice casino."

"Majority shares, my love. Congratulations."

She blinked up at him. "You bought Bobby's casino for me?"

"Most of it," he said. "But Bobby still has a stake. What fun would it be if you couldn't torture him a bit?"

Cara laughed. "Oh, my God, you mean I'm Bobby Gold's boss?"

"If you'd like the other casinos, I'll get them for you."

She shook her head. "No, one is enough." Ridiculously, her eyes filled with tears. "Thank you."

Jack set the tray aside and pushed her back against the pillows. "Just think, every year on the anniversary of our first meeting, we can close the high-stakes room and play our very own game, just the two of us."

"What did you have in mind?" Cara asked as his lips found the pulse in her throat.

His sinfully sexy laugh vibrated against her neck. "Strip poker, of course."

* * * * *

LARGER-PRINT BOOKS!

GET 2 FREE LARGER-PRINT NOVELS PLUS 2 FREE GIFTS!

YES! Please send me 2 FREE LARGER-PRINT Harlequin Presents® novels and my 2 FREE gifts (gifts are worth about $10). After receiving them, if I don't wish to receive any more books, I can return the shipping statement marked "cancel". If I don't cancel, I will receive 6 brand-new novels every month and be billed just $4.80 per book in the U.S. or $5.49 per book in Canada. That's a saving of at least 13% off the cover price! It's quite a bargain! Shipping and handling is just 50¢ per book in the U.S. and 75¢ per book in Canada.* I understand that accepting the 2 free books and gifts places me under no obligation to buy anything. I can always return a shipment and cancel at any time. Even if I never buy another book, the two free books and gifts are mine to keep forever.

176/376 HDN FER2

Name	(PLEASE PRINT)
Address	Apt. #
City	State/Prov. Zip/Postal Code

Signature (if under 18, a parent or guardian must sign)

Mail to the **Reader Service:**
IN U.S.A.: P.O. Box 1867, Buffalo, NY 14240-1867
IN CANADA: P.O. Box 609, Fort Erie, Ontario L2A 5X3

Not valid for current subscribers to Harlequin Presents Larger-Print books.

**Are you a subscriber to Harlequin Presents books
and want to receive the larger-print edition?
Call 1-800-873-8635 today or visit us at www.ReaderService.com.**

* Terms and prices subject to change without notice. Prices do not include applicable taxes. Sales tax applicable in N.Y. Canadian residents will be charged applicable taxes. Offer not valid in Quebec. This offer is limited to one order per household. All orders subject to credit approval. Credit or debit balances in a customer's account(s) may be offset by any other outstanding balance owed by or to the customer. Please allow 4 to 6 weeks for delivery. Offer available while quantities last.

Your Privacy—The Reader Service is committed to protecting your privacy. Our Privacy Policy is available online at www.ReaderService.com or upon request from the Reader Service.

We make a portion of our mailing list available to reputable third parties that offer products we believe may interest you. If you prefer that we not exchange your name with third parties, or if you wish to clarify or modify your communication preferences, please visit us at www.ReaderService.com/consumerschoice or write to us at Reader Service Preference Service, P.O. Box 9062, Buffalo, NY 14269. Include your complete name and address.

HPLP11B